Dedication

To Georgina and Michael.
Thank you.

M.E. Ellington

THE MARTIALIS
INCIDENT

AUSTIN MACAULEY PUBLISHERS™

LONDON • CAMBRIDGE • NEW YORK • SHARJAH

A CIP catalogue record for this title is available from the British Library.

ISBN: 978-1-78710-745-8 (Paperback)
ISBN: 978-1-78710-746-5 (E-Book)
www.austinmacauley.com

First Published (2017)
Austin Macauley Publishers Ltd.™
25 Canada Square
Canary Wharf
London
E14 5LQ

Acknowledgments

To my Editor, Steven D Stiefel

I would like to thank Steven for his help and guidance
with this book.

Magnetosphere

An asymmetrical region surroundings the earth, beginning about 100 km (62 miles) above the surface on the side of the earth facing the Sun and extending hundreds of thousands of kilometers into space on the opposite side. In this region, the earth's magnetic field exerts a significant influence on any charged particles that encounter it. The magnetosphere deflects most of the charged particles in the solar wind, but also traps and deflects some of these particles toward the earth's magnetic poles, causing magnetic storms and auroras.

Coronal Mass Ejection

A massive, bubble-shaped burst of plasma expanding outward from the Sun's corona, in which large amounts of superheated particles are emitted at almost the speed of light. The emissions can cause disturbances in the solar wind that disrupt satellites and create powerful magnetic storms on earth. The flow of the solar wind sometimes interferes with the operation of artificial satellites, electronic communications and electric power transmission on the earth.

Asphyxia

Obstruction of air flow resulting in hypoxia severe enough to cause unconsciousness, hypercapnia, hypoxemia, and, if not treated immediately, death.

Prologue
What's to Come

What do you see when look to our Sun? Do you see the giver of heat, of light and of life? And what of the countless stars in the night sky? Millions of Suns all emanating their life-giving heat and light across the vastness of space. Some stars are no longer alive, their light extinguished millions of years ago, but only now reaching us on earth.

In the early part of the 21st century, few people thought about the Sun. Consumed with the wars across the African continent and the Middle East, the increasing posturing from Russia, and with the real threats from global warming, mankind looked inward and focused on the earthly threats to our way of life. There were men who observed the night sky for the cosmological bodies that would bring destruction to our planet. These objects have visited our planet before. And they will again.

But, few men considered a threat from our own Sun, which has risen and set over our planet since the dawn of time. Few men contemplated that with all of the threats which we have made by our own hands, that it would be our own Sun which would turn from being the bringer of life, to become the harbinger of death. And for all of our technology, and our great achievements, we would be powerless against one of the mightiest forces in the universe.

Part One
The First Signs

McGill Artic Research Station (M.A.R.S) North Pole

February 5th, 2023

The station lay in ruins, and its staff dead; asphyxiated as they tried to flee the crawling death which now surrounded and enveloped the station. Where the comms. building once stood, a crashed helicopter, sent to rescue them after their desperate cry for help, lay in a debris field of its own making. But there was no fire, the aviation fuel, normally so flammable, pooled by the crash site.

What had taken place here happened without warning, and it was quick. Too quick for the experienced team to react and save themselves. But perhaps more worryingly, it happened with such speed, they had no time to send out a warning.

For now, what had occurred here would remain a mystery. Eventually, it would have ramifications for us all.

Part Two
The Event: Two Years Earlier

Chapter 1
"Ladies and Gentlemen and, of course, the Press"

April 28th, 2021.

A muted and somewhat polite chuckle was heard from the gathered crowd inside the main hangar of the Kennedy Space Center, as flight director Bruce McCaughey started his speech. The audience had gathered in the huge hangar to hear the details of the Martialis project, the first manned mission to Mars. Fold away chairs were laid out in neat rows, with names painstakingly attached to them. The more important you were considered to be; the closer you were to the front. Here a temporary stage had been set up, with a long table running beneath it. Bruce McCaughey stood on the stage to their right, and grasped the black and chrome pulpit. His well-rehearsed speech resonated throughout the hollow steel structure.

"Since man first gazed at the stars in wonderment, we have strived to understand the universe around us, and our place in it. But for all we've learned, for all we have expanded our knowledge, the one constant, the one celestial body, that has always caught our imagination is the planet Mars. We look upon it with a strange curiosity as we are drawn to it, as if we are looking at where we came from. And though we have sent probes to that far-off planet, and collected mountains of data, we have yet to have that tangible experience. Now we have evidence of running water it is more important than ever that we stand on Mars as a united people. I can announce that on September 23rd this year, a crew of five will begin their journey to Mars. Once they arrive, they will answer the biggest question we have ever faced. Did life once flourish on Mars? And if it did, what happened? Ladies and gentlemen, without further delay, it is my great honor to introduce the crew that will take that giant step for mankind, please welcome; Commander Jake Iverson of the U.S. Air Force, Chun Yue from the Chinese National Space Administration, Joe Jamison of the Royal Air Force, Sergey Zorin from the Russian Federal Space Agency, and Mary Duval from the European Space Agency."

Bruce then turned to the large screen that hung above the table. On it was a live feed from the International Space Station where Commander Relford sat waiting. "I'd also like to introduce Commander Relford who's aboard the ISS. His team will be instrumental to the mission, once it leaves earth's atmosphere."

Applause began as the five crew members made their entrance from behind the massive U.S. and Chinese flags that hung behind the stage. Next to it hung the flags of the Great Britain, Russia and France. Although they were all the same size, the Chinese and U.S. flag hung slightly higher as if re-affirming the point that the U.S. and China were the only countries that could jointly afford to fund the development of the new propulsion system which had allowed this mission to become a reality. Bruce McCaughey waved the astronauts onto the stage where they took their seats behind the long desk. The questions began.

Alice Fisher, a slim smart suited woman with long brown hair tied in a ponytail asked the first question. "Commander Iverson, how does it feel to be the first human to travel to Mars?"

Jake Iverson leaned forward to meet his microphone. Jake was the all-American hero, 6'1 he was athletically thin but powerfully built. He had short dark hair clipped into a military *no fuss stay-neat style*. His facial features matched the rest of him: a well-defined chin sat below a straight nose and steely green eyes and around them the few wrinkles of a well-travelled and experienced man, who seemed to ooze confidence, even before he spoke.

"Well, Miss Fisher, as you can see by my crew, this is an international mission, with each country represented here bringing with it the best qualified and most able to accomplish their part of this mission." He smiled at her and turned away to field the next question. Alice smiled to herself; she'd already had inside information from her source that all was not what it appeared to be. But she knew that here, in front of the worlds' press and with the commander of the ISS on a live link, it would be nothing but a controlled and well-rehearsed public relations exercise.

A Canadian news reporter was the next to speak. "This question is for Commander Relford on board the ISS. Commander Relford, Bruce has told us that your team will be vital to this mission. Can you explain that?" he asked.

After a few seconds delay Commander Relford answered. "Yes, once the ship leaves the gravitational pull of the earth it will sling shot around our planet using the earth's gravity to gain momentum. My crew and I will work with Commander Iverson and the crew of SOL 1 to ensure that they're just where they need to be, which is above Antarctica."

"Why is that so vital?" the news reporter asked.

There were a few more seconds of delay. "Well because of their trajectory they will fire the new fission engines over the South Pole where they will pass closest to our atmosphere. Using our guidance systems with those on SOL 1, we can be much more accurate because we're out of the earth's atmosphere," he answered.

The questions came fast and furious. "Joe, or is it Joseph? Robert Powell, BBC. How does the propulsion system enable this mission to be possible, when previous rocket powered craft could not provide the speed and long-distance propulsion necessary for a return trip to Mars?"

In the same way Jake looked like a picture book American astronaut, Joe Jamison looked like the typical, highly trained professional, of the Royal Air Force. He was as tall as Jake, but a thicker, more powerful build. His hair had almost all gone, what was left was clipped down to nothing but a small patch of stubble close to his ears, meeting at the back of his head. He leaned towards his microphone, folding his arms and looking at the questioner.

"The theory is simple. Our system uses nuclear fusion, the same as the sun. This allows for a much more sustainable power supply, which is also much lighter. This means we don't need as much fuel payload to break free of the earth's gravity. It will dramatically increase our speed, and that's what will enable us to make the journey to Mars in months, allowing us to remain on the surface for as long as 30 months, much longer than previously thought possible."

The questions continued: the usual questions about the morality of finding out things we might later regret, or should never discover, crept up as they expected they would. As well as the other hot topics of what effect the power system would have on earth's already delicate climate, and whether the costs could be justified. But the well briefed and rehearsed crew glided through them with ease. Until it was time to reveal the spacecraft itself.

With great pride, Flight Director Bruce McCaughey pulled the lever. The large flags slid to one side revealing the craft.

Mounted upright, this ship was smaller but far more impressive than anything before it. Looking like something the team at NASA had lifted straight from the pages of some Star Trek fanzine, it was more impressive than anything that had come before. As the ship came into full view, the applause started again. And once again they died down to a slow single clap, as Bruce stepped forward to explain the functionality of the ship. He stood holding his arms outright towards the massive ship.

"I give you SOL 1, the most advanced piece of technology on our planet and soon to be on another. At the front, you can see the flight deck, behind that is the science stations and bathrooms, behind that is the crew's area where they will take turns to sleep, eat and exercise. The large section behind that is the cargo hold which will allow them to bring back samples from Mars, and at the tail end is the propulsion system and engines."

The questions continued.

"Mark Goldberg, from NCC News. You mentioned the propulsion system relies on nuclear fusion. Do you know if that will have any effects on climate or atmosphere?"

Sergey Zorin leaned into his microphone, smiling as he did. Sergey had spent most of his adult life living and working between Russia and the U.S. graduating from MIT with honors. He'd returned home to Dmitrov, a small town an hour or so from Moscow, before accepting a post with the Russian Federal Space Agency as a propulsion specialist. Sergey's command of the English language was excellent, and without an accent. A thin man, he stood 6'5", with dark short hair and deep-set brown eyes, which sat sharply against the pale complexion of his thin drawn face. He stretched out a large hand and cradled the microphone stand.

"The propulsion system we are using will have no effect on either the climate or the atmosphere of the earth. We have tested the system both inside a controlled setting and outside, and we have measured no effects to the local environment, thank you." He leaned back smiling, first at Mark Goldberg, and then to the crew with an obvious expression of relief.

Bruce walked the stage, "Any further questions?"

Alice Fisher rose from her seat again. "I know that the space agencies involved are reluctant to release the exact cost of this mission, but given that the world economy is fragile, I would like to ask if it can be justified?"

Bruce smiled, "I think Miss Mary Duval from the European Space Agency is best qualified to answer that specific question, Miss Fisher." Bruce turned to his right and gestured a hand towards her.

Mary leaned into her microphone and cleared her throat. She was a graceful woman, self-confident in an under stated, and dignified manner, her short brown hair was elegant and practical. The smallest of the crew at a mere 5'4, she was slim and wore the standardized uniform much better than the designers had ever imagined it would be. Living and working in Paris, the headquarters of the European Space Agency, she had mastered English as well as Sergey, but she still spoke it with an ever-present accent.

"Thank you, Bruce. The question of where we came from is our oldest question, and yet it is still principally unanswered. This mission may well provide the answer that could unite mankind like never before, and perhaps end all wars, many of which are based on cultural differences regarding religion and our origin. We also must consider the potential resource implications. If a permanent colony can be established on Mars, then we would use such a place as a launching pad, to travel farther out, to look for resources that our own planet is running out of."

With that Bruce called an end to the proceedings, and thanked everyone for attending. As the last of the audience meandered from the hangar, the crew members made their way through to the family room, where a buffet of traditional foods from countries of each astronaut was set out. Bruce walked toward the huddle of the crew and their families that had made the trip for the big news conference and the reveal of the ship. He turned to Mary.

"Well handled Mary. I knew that woman would bring something like that up, she always tries to make us squirm."

"It was no problem Bruce," she replied smiling.

Bruce cracked a smile in the corner of his mouth. Mary had once again, with ease, disarmed a statement meant to provoke a response. Nodding, he turned his attentions to Jake and Joe, who were standing with their families.

"Hey guys, good stuff up there." Bruce smiled, as he approached.

The polite conversation carried on for an hour, before one by one, the crew members made their excuses and left. As Bruce stood with Jake, who as usual was the last to leave, mission specialist Steve David approached them. Steve had worked on this mission since its inception eight years ago, and had continuously voiced his concerns over the experimental propulsion system when they decided it would be used.

Though nuclear fusion was the energy that powers the universe, its effects on a planet's atmosphere could never be completely tested. All of the testing had been theoretical computer models and simulations and some of them had showed worrying outcomes. But in NASA's rush to move the space program on after it was halted, following the financial crash of 2008 and the subsequent global financial crisis, the parameters of the testing were altered to produce safe results.

"Bruce, do you have a minute?" Steve asked.

"Yes, please excuse me Jake."

"No problem sir," Jake replied.

"This way." Bruce pointed Steve toward the small offices that lined the hangar.

Steve followed him into the end office and sat opposite him. "I've being going over the original tests and I still don't think we should continue with this launch until we have tested the propulsion systems further," he said.

Bruce smiled, but it was frustration, not friendliness. "I understand your worries Steve."

Steve interrupted him. "I don't think you do, I'm the mission specialist, if I think it's unsafe to proceed then you know I can call a stop to the mission!" he said, defiantly.

Bruce's expression changed. "This mission will go ahead with or without you. I appreciate your worries and concerns and they're well known but make no mistake. You cause any ripples with this, you will be fired. Now if you'll excuse me." Bruce stood and left the office closing the door behind him.

Once he was sure Bruce was out of sight Steve pulled his cell phone from his pocket and called his long-time friend Jacob Miller. They had worked together on this mission, and while Steve had stayed in the thick of it, being involved with the mission conception and development, Jacob had taken a different path. His expertise had become the studying and collating of data. Though they worked from different facilities and in different roles they had kept in touch and Steve now saw him as a confidante, someone he could trust and turn to on matters like these, even though he knew Jacob had no influence. But he needed to talk to someone.

He pressed Jacob's speed dial, and it answered, "Hi Jacob, it's me, ya got a minute?"

"Sure," Jacob replied.

"I've spoken to Bruce about these earlier test results but he doesn't want to know. He's threatened to fire me if I don't keep my mouth shut about this."

"Then you need to keep quiet Steve, the President himself pushed this through to get us to Mars. If you fuck this up they won't just fire you, they'll ruin you," Jacob warned him.

"But this propulsion system is untested in the real-world Jacob. We have no clue if it will affect our climate or even the atmosphere." Steve pushed the point home, becoming more troubled as he spoke.

"Yeah, I know, but there is no facility that can recreate an atmosphere like earths. It has to be simulations. It can't be real-world-tested. You know that. Just hope it passes without incident my friend."

"Do I have a choice?" Steve asked, knowing what the answer would be.

"No, no you don't."

Steve pushed the *end-call* button on his phone and sighed as he pushed his cell phone back into his pocket, knowing Jacob was right. If he pushed this, and went public with it, his career, and his life would be over. He'd never work in engineering again, and especially space engineering, even if it was in the private sector. There was no choice but to look the other way and tow the official line. Feeling defeated and as if he'd let himself down he left the office.

The months that had once seemed to stretch out before them, were now gone in the blink of an eye, and launch day was now only one week away. With the long-range weather report favorable, and all systems reporting one hundred percent readiness, there seemed no reason the historical, experimental launch should not go ahead.

September 23rd, 8:43 a.m.

Bruce stood at his post in the control room. The time to launch now stood at two hours, seventeen minutes and thirty-two seconds.

The crew already aboard SOL 1 concentrated upon their individual roles. As commander, Jake had the most to focus on. He was responsible for the safety of the crew and of the ship and the success of the mission. As his first officer, Joe was second in command, and would take on some of Jake's responsibilities once the mission had begun. Sergey was the engineer and the mission propulsion specialist. As environment and ecology specialist, Mary's role would be vital once they had touched down on Mars.

That was when Mary would take control of the mission, setting up of the bio domes and living quarters. But any critical decisions would still sit on Jake's shoulders. Navigation and life support fell to Chun Yue, a Chinese national who studied at Oxford before returning to China.

He'd been handpicked by the heads of the Chinese space program because of his familiarity with Anglos. He was the quietest of the group, proficiently going about his duties. As with Sergey, Chun Yue's command of the English language was excellent, though it did have some Mandarin inflections.

"Are we all strapped in, and ready boys and girls?" Jake asked with an affectionate tone. As the commander, Jake not only saw himself as the group's leader, but also as a surrogate father, the oldest of the team, and the one that they could, and should come to if they encounter a problem.

The large countdown clock that hung on the wall of the control room in mission control now read, zero hours, eighteen minutes, fifty-one seconds, and the atmosphere inside the control room had changed. Each person in the control room understood their own part which they'd rehearsed over and over, and not just during the training sessions but in their sleep, while driving to work and in the shower. Long gone was the sense of confidence and self-assuredness they had all once enjoyed. Now was the time for a million *what if, and have we* questions that everybody was trying to answer. Any mistakes, any oversights now would put any future manned missions to Mars back decades and that was something that could not be allowed to happen. Not with so much dependent on this mission.

Bruce's mind raced as he tried to cover every aspect of this mission. He glanced over to where Steve David sat. Bruce had feared that he would be the one that might have ended this mission by voicing his concerns over the propulsion system. So far, he'd kept quiet and Bruce was confident he would continue to do so. But just in case he didn't Steve's cell phone, landline and email accounts were hacked after he'd threatened to go public at the press conference back in April. Steve had, for the most part, followed his usual routine, which as he lived alone meant more time than most at work and the odd meeting with

Jacob Miller, though Bruce paid no attention to this as Jacob also worked for NASA. The rest of his time he spent playing console games and watching TV. Bruce's drifting thoughts and concerns about Steve came back to the here and now as the control room's buzz picked up and became tangible. The counting clock would not wait for Bruce to clear any concerns and the countdown continued. Zero hours, seven minutes and twenty-five seconds. To Bruce now, and to all of them in the control room, time seemed to speed up, drawing them closer to the point of no return. The experienced among them knew that when that point came, time would then play its ultimate trick. It would stand still, making every second feel like an hour until SOL 1 was clear of the earth's atmosphere, and the green lights across the board confirmed that all was okay. Zero hours, one minute and fifty-three seconds.

"Jake. How's things?" Bruce called him for the final check.

"Looking good here Bruce, ready for our Sunday drive." Jake replied with the same relaxed confidence he'd shown since project Martialis began.

"All clear here Jake. Looks like you're going today Buddy."

"Sure, hope so Bruce, we're all packed and the kids are eager to go to Mars."

All stations reported green across the board, and the last few seconds of the countdown began.

"We have lift off, of the Martialis manned mission to Mars. God speed to SOL 1 and her crew."

SOL 1 rose gracefully from her launch pad. The fusion engines produced little of the thunder and drama of the previous rocket engines, and no water was needed to cool the launch area, so there was none of the usual plumes of super-heated steam. There were no rumblings or vibrations from the ground up to the flight deck. With little noise and fuss, and with little effort, SOL 1 glided from the ground and into a high earth orbit for one pass around before heading off towards Mars.

Bruce walked over to where Steve sat and leaned over to whisper to him, "See, no problems!"

"SOL 1 has launched successfully. We can confirm all systems are go." Jake's voice came over the comms.

"Affirmative, Jake. We're all good down here too. See you in three years buddy, God speed to you all, over," Bruce replied, as he smiled to Steve.

Chapter 2
Titusville Florida
(Near the Kennedy Space Center)

January 12th, 2022.

Alice awoke in another hotel bedroom, to the sound of her favorite music track repeating on a short cycle. Pushing her long dark hair from her face she knew by the tune that this call was from a friend or family member. Her work ring tone was a different song, and one she often wanted to ignore but never did. She pushed back the thick duvet and reached over to the night stand. She picked up the phone. The screen read Rob, Alice's former husband of six years. She lay back on the bed with the phone in front of her, her thumb hanging over the green *Answer* button trying to decide what to do. Pressing the Red *Ignore* button the phone once again became silent, and she put it back on to the night stand.

"Who was that?" The voice came from the en-suite bathroom.

"No one important," Alice answered.

The door opened and Jacob Miller stepped out, the large complimentary white towel wrapped around his waist. Jacob and Alice had met when she'd been covering the Martialis mission, the previous year. One of the lead data scientists at NASA, he'd taken a special interest in Alice, giving her tours of the facility that no other reporter had the privilege of seeing. He wasn't a traditional-handsome looking man, nor was he well built; he was in fact what a rocket scientist would look like if you are asked to describe one. But as Alice had spent time with him on the project, she had become attracted to him and his easy-going ways. Alice couldn't pinpoint just when the dynamic had changed between them, and she'd spent many a waking hour thinking about it, but their relationship had transitioned faster than she might have expected. There was no pretense of them falling forlornly in love. Alice had only left Rob a few months before they met and she wasn't ready for another committed relationship. She'd made that clear to Jacob. They both understood that this relationship was about fun and release, and as Jacob had often said, "The brightest and most intense stars burn out fastest." But that was last year, and as Alice had spent more time in the U.S. covering the ongoing mission she'd spent more time with Jacob, and feelings had developed. Feelings she knew could be dangerous.,

"Good," Jacob said, smiling as he walked back across the small room toward the bed. Jacob was of average height with a slim build, but he wasn't a skinny man, he had short dark hair and he always had a shadow of facial hair.

Alice smiled back at him and watched as he dressed.

"What're your plans today?" she asked him as he tucked in his plain white office shirt into his dark blue chinos.

"Oh, nothing much, we're reviewing the launch of SOL 1 to see if there were any effects we hadn't noticed first time around. It'll be routine and boring I'm sure."

"Such as?"

Jacob smiled, "You know I can't discuss that with you."

Alice moved to the end of the bed and grabbed him around his waist. "You're not leaving until you give me something," she said, tickling him.

He fell backward on the bed and grabbed her, "I gave you something last night, didn't I?" he replied.

"Uh, I could have gotten that from anyone," she teased him.

"Okay, okay but this stays between us," Jacob said; now lying out on the bed with Alice sat across him.

She climbed off him and sat next to him. "Sounds interesting?"

"We weren't sure how the new propulsion system would react with the earth's atmosphere, we'd run simulations but we weren't one hundred-percent sure. A friend of mine, well a colleague, raised concerns, but he was ordered to keep quiet."

"And no one knows about this?"

"No, no one other than Bruce and me and Steve. That's his name, Steve David," Jacob replied.

"Well what did he think would happen?"

"He didn't that's the point. We didn't know, but it's been four months since the launch and we have noticed nothing, so I guess it's all good."

"So, his doubts were unfounded then?" she asked again.

Jacob smiled and changed the subject. "What about you? What's your world changing assignment?" Jacob retaliated.

"Ugh, don't ask. Our normal political journo is away on vacation so they want me to cover a diplomat from Gaza. He's here *to try* and bring about lasting peace between Israel and Palestine which they say could lead to the end of I.S." Alice's head slumped back on the pillow as if to exaggerate just how boring she found political journalism. She much preferred her own field, the scientific interest stories.

Jacob laughed at her frustration. "Don't be like that. You might be there when history is made, and a final and everlasting piece is brokered."

"Yeah, and it's more likely I'll be there when they can't agree, and keep on fighting as usual. Fucking religion!"

Jacob, now dressed, turned and looked at Alice after he'd reached the door. He smiled and blew her a kiss. "Cheer up. Boring news means we're all safe for another day."

After he left, Alice sighed and thought about getting up to shower. She'd have to catch a flight to Washington. If she wasn't there in the morning to cover the diplomat, the shit would hit the fan. She followed her usual routine of showering, drying her hair and applying just the right balance of makeup. Not so much that she looked ready for a night on the town, but just enough to make her look professional and feel confident. She packed her overnight bag and left for the flight that would take her to Washington, and another hotel, where she would stay in an almost identical room from the one she'd just left. It seemed the only thing that separated hotels were the view from the bedroom window, and as this was one of her many visits to this hotel, found on Maryland Avenue, she knew that the view would include a part of the Washington Monument and the Lincoln Memorial at the opposite end of the reflecting pool.

The flight along the East Coast was routine and mundane, with just a little excitement when two NTSB officers boarded. She overheard the older man calling the young officer Simon. Much to her relief, the plane touched down in Washington. Alice made her way to the hotel, where she had her favorite meal of a green salad and sweet-chili chicken, served in her room where she could slip out of her business suit and put on her tracksuit bottoms and t-shirt before resting on the bed and bringing the large flat screen to life. She smiled to herself at the thought of the alternatives. Her one-time visit to a reunion site where she'd searched for people from her school had made her feel somewhat lucky. The majority of the girls had settled for the married life, playing mum and dutiful housewife, living within a five-mile area of where they themselves were born and raised. Some weren't working at all, though in the current economic climate, and cataclysmic effect on the UK economy that the policies the Coalition Government had followed, that didn't surprise her.

Night soon closed in and brought to an end another cold snow-filled day on the Eastern Seaboard. The hotel, as always, was kept to a warm and inviting temperature, and Alice soon decided to turn in for an early night. Relaxing under the heavy duvet, she flicked through the endless channels finding nothing she wanted to watch. As she finally gave in, and twitched off the TV her phone replayed her favorite tune.

"Hello Rob," Alice answered.

"Hi, how are you? I called you this morning but you didn't answer." Rob's question came quick, but much to her delight and relief, it also came with no tone of inquisition.

"You called while I was in the shower, then I was in a rush to get my plane. I meant to call after I landed in Washington."

"Washington? Wow you are getting around America!"

"You know me darling, always on the move. Anyway, how are the little cherubs?" Alice asked about their children, changing the subject from work.

Rob and Alice had two children, twin boys Ben and Max, aged three. Ben and Max had come along nine years after they had met, and six years after they had wed. It was always their plan they would have children. Alice wanted a large family, but after the twin's birth, and still only aged 33, Rob had developed aggressive testicular cancer. The treatment had saved his life but he could no longer have children, or any kind of a sex life, and while Alice hated herself for it she couldn't help resenting Rob. It was as if she felt he was responsible for his own illness, though she knew that wasn't true. But what made her feel even worse was that she used Rob's illness along with her reasoning to justify her leaving him and finding comfort with Jacob. It seemed easier to blame Rob than to judge herself.

The last time they had been out as a family was the previous year. Alice had returned home before the launch of SOL 1, and at the end of August they had spent an idyllic day having a picnic close to a small village located not far from Warwick. The boys had played close by while Alice and Rob had lay with each other on the tartan rug they'd brought along. The then still married couple gazed at the deep blue sky that contrasted with the bright green leaves of the overhanging trees. She remembered the slow summer breeze that now and again swept across them, providing cool, soft relief from the heat of the sun. She remembered the feelings of completeness and fulfilment that had left her alone for so long after Rob had become ill, but the guilt returned as she remembered that it was also how she felt while she was with Jacob. Rob's voice brought her back.

"Ben and Max are fine, they're in bed now. They're up to their usual tricks, you know, boys will be boys." The nervous false laugh returned.

"I'm glad to hear it. How are they coping with nursery?" Alice needed to change the conversation. Rob's laugh was making her anxious.

"Good, yeah they're doing well. Max, of course, has taken to it like a duck to water. And Ben is a little unsure, but he likes the new teacher so that's a big plus I guess."

"I'm glad to hear that." Alice had now run out of things to talk about.

Rob continued, "Why are you in Washington? Anything good or exciting?"

"No. The paper wants me to cover a diplomat; he's coming to meet the President," Alice answered.

"That's serious stuff." Rob tried to expand the conversation with a compliment.

"I guess," Alice answered, her voice becoming duller.

"Have things in the U.S. changed much?"

Alice changed the subject, trying to hurry the conversation along. "Well so long as you're okay," she said, as she pushed her fingers through her now tangled hair. The inevitable awkward silence followed as they both tried to finish the call. As Alice drew a breath to do so Rob spoke.

"I called to check in, call me later when you know your plans, and when you'll be home."

"Will do."

Alice stared at her phone's bright screen for a moment before she tossed it onto the bed and collapsed back down into the heavy warm sheets. Things with Rob hadn't been the same since his illness. They'd had big plans; they would have a family young and travel around the world, enjoy the things that would have seemed like a fantasy when they were growing up. Technology and global markets now allowed for this kind of thinking. There was no need to stay in the area of your upbringing anymore. But that idyllic world they had built for each other in their minds had come crashing down with the diagnosis of the cancer.

The posting to the U.S. was now the best she could hope for. She'd grabbed the opportunity when it had come along. She understood if she'd turned it down nothing else would have been offered. Rob's health was better, but his career as a leading architect had gone. He did some work from home, helping his former employers with technicalities when they needed his expertise, but his life now was with the boys, and whilst he continued to suffer from chronic fatigue, another effect of the cancer and treatment; it was all he might manage. A single tear fell down Alice's face and she fell into a deep warm sleep.

The morning started as all hotel mornings start, with the buzz of the alarm and then the early call from the polite and over enthusiastic alarm call. Alice hauled herself from her bed after a restless night of self-doubt and guilt, followed by reconciliations over her situation. She showered, preened and dressed and headed down for breakfast, walking past the wall mounted TV, which was broadcasting live images from the Martialis mission on Mars. Alice helped herself to the continental breakfast bar, checking the time to make sure she did not miss the arrival of the diplomat. After breakfast, she walked through the lobby, and past a small crowd of people who had gathered around the TV.

As she passed, taking no notice, the large screen flashed red writing across the bottom.

** Breaking News: Contact with the Martialis mission lost: more to follow**

Alice waved a taxi, and asked to be taken to the press area of the White House where she would meet up with her photographer. The paper used this freelance photographer whenever it needed coverage in the Washington area. Though Alice had only met him once when she was covering the previous Presidential elections, they had kept in contact through social media.

"Hey Alice." A young voice caught her attention; it was Brent, only just out of his internship with a local photographer

"Hi Brent."

"Hey Alice," he called again and continued, "How are you? You haven't changed, still a yummy mummy," Brent said, as he laughed.

"Wow, look at you, you've blown up," she replied, smiling.

"What can I tell you, been hitting the gym hard."

"Looks good on you."

Brent took the digital SLR from his kit back. He attached the lens and took his position on the platform with other photographers, who now jostled and pushed to get the best picture.

"Brent, here comes the limo." Alice shouted up to him from her position just behind the metal barrier.

As the large black bullet proof limousine stopped along with the police and secret service escort, a tall broad man in a dark blue suit opened the diplomat's door. Noise from the cameras and shutters drowned out almost all other background noises. An anti-climax of these things was more-or-less guaranteed. Once he was ushered inside the motorcade sped away, leaving the journalists and photographers to gather their belongings and leave.

"Did you get the shots Brent?" Alice asked as he re-joined her by the barrier.

"Yeah, what there was to get. I'll email them to the office tonight."

"Until next time then," Alice said with a smile.

Alice headed towards her usual haunt, a coffee shop inside the Ronald Reagan building on Pennsylvanian Avenue Northwest. The shop offered Alice what she needed; a coffee, warmth and Wi-Fi, allowing her to write her report on the arrival and then email it to her editor back in London. It always sounded so easy when summed up, but with her inbuilt boredom of politics, she found herself once again staring at a blank screen with a cursor waiting in the top left corner, flashing like an eager dog wagging its tale while it waits. After agonizing and correcting, and then correcting the corrections, and five coffees and two pastries later, she hit the send button in her email and the attached word document left her screen

Back in the hotel bedroom Alice changed into something she could relax in, and settled in for night. But before she allowed herself to relax too much she had to call her boss, and she had some news she knew he'd be interested in. She dialed his cell and waited for his usual answer. She didn't have to wait long.

"Mike Watson." Mike was Alice's immediate boss and the editor of the paper she worked for. He was in his late fifties, short and overweight, with a temper to match his own disappointments in life.

"Hi Mike."

"Hi Alice. What can I do for you?" he asked, bluntly.

"As usual, straight to the point."

"Alice, I don't have time for anything else."

"My source at NASA has told me that the propulsion system they used wasn't fully tested."

"Say that again," he said, now sounding interested.

"Exactly, he said someone there, a guy by the name of Steve David had concerns about the safety of it, he was worried what effect it might have on our atmosphere, but he was told if he blabbed he would be fired."

"Is this credible?" Mike asked.

"Yes, without a doubt."

"Okay, stay on it and get me more information on this Steve David, and put a piece together. We'll go to NASA for their comments before we publish it."

"See, I'm not just a pretty face, am I?" Alice said.

"Write the piece, then I'll tell you."

Alice ended the call and plugged her cell phone into its charger before placing it on the night stand as she climbed into bed. As she fell asleep, warm and safe from the winter's night, she, like the rest of the world, had no idea of what was to come.

Chapter 3

February 20th, 2022

SOL1 and her crew had arrived on Mars as planned in December, and by January they had set up the habitat they would call home for the next twenty-four months. The main body and propulsion system of SOL 1 circled above the red planet in a geo stationary orbit, while the lander had become the central hub for their otherworldly camping trip, with the lander itself as the nerve center, housing the components and instruments needed to measure and record the results of all 128 experiments of this mission. The first section that reached out from the central hub, housed the hydroponics for the phototrophic organisms, essential not only for supplementing the stocks of food, but also sustaining oxygen levels. This was also where the communications center was. It was here that they would talk with mission control and with their families via a secured video call. The second housed their living quarters, complete with beds, a small gym, food prep area, toilet and sonic shower, and a flat screen TV which included a library of movies and music, as well a data bank of images to remind them of home.

For Jacob, it was just another Friday on earth in the offices at the Kennedy Space Center, and as usual he was pouring over the terabytes of data collected by the crew of SOL 1 on their journey to Mars. Jacob had had no real face-time with the astronauts since their departure. He had met them when they were selected for the mission and everyone concerned had been invited to a *meet and greet*. But soon after this he found himself in the background, doing the real work of studying the thousands of sensor readings and data sent back during the journey to the red planet, and the first few weeks of their stay. Jacob took a sip from his coffee and returned to his desk. It was late, very late, and he was the last one at his post. The data sent back from Mars was far greater in both detail and substance than anybody had expected, but as budget changes had cut deeper, no extra staff had been brought in to help. It was down to Jacob and his few remaining colleagues. Stationed by a large window, his desk overlooked the all-but-empty parking lot. A mist had crawled over the empty cars. He shuddered a little at the thought of leaving his warm office, took another sip of his coffee and turned back to his computer screen.

He tabbed between the open windows on his desktop, and found a new report that had just arrived in his personal inbox. Jacob was puzzled. Why would an internal report be sent to my personal inbox he thought to himself? It was a low status report, something that wouldn't have been picked up by the server's monitoring systems and probably something Jacob would have passed over had it come through his work inbox. His hand hovered over the icon on his touch-screen for a while as he decided whether to open it. Fuck-it, he thought to himself as he opened the attached file. The attachment opened and filled the screen. *ATMOS*. The title page showed a total page count of 258. Jacob sighed; he was too tired to look at it now. He took another sip and pressed the print icon for the personal printer which sat on his desk. Normally any documents would be sent to the general office printer for ease.

But something niggled him about this. And though he suspected that the file had been sent to the wrong inbox in error, he decided to keep it to himself until he'd read it. As the laser printer started up, Jacob picked up his cell phone and car keys and left the office.

The drive home was as always uneventful. Jacob lived only a few miles from the Kennedy Space Center in Port St John. But when he arrived he could see another car parked in his driveway and he recognized it immediately, it belonged to his friend Steve David. Jacob was tired, but he was glad of the company. He stopped his car and climbed out to see Steve standing outside his house huddled against the mist which was now turning to a fine rain. Jacob smiled and waved as he locked his car.

"Hi Steve, this is unexpected."

"Is it?" Steve asked.

"Come in, out of this weather."

Steve followed Jacob inside and as Jacob switched on the lights, Steve took one last look outside and then pushed the door closed before sitting down. It was clear to Jacob that something was wrong; he could tell by Steve's body language that something was bothering him.

"What's up?" Jacob asked.

"I was fired today!"

"Why?" Jacob had an uneasy feeling about what the answer might be.

"Because a London newspaper ran a story about how NASA is concerned about the propulsion system of SOL 1, and that it hadn't been *fully* tested. They're blaming me for the leak, I'm fucking ruined and it's your fault!"

"Mine! How the hell is this my fault?" Jacob snapped back.

"Because apart from Bruce, you're the only one I fucking told!"

"How the hell would I tell a newspaper this? And why?" Jacob defended himself.

"You told that little bitch *Alice*, didn't you? And she printed it. Do you know what this has done to me, and to my reputation?" Steve was becoming upset.

"I hardly see her."

"Come on Jacob everyone knows you're screwing her, don't play games. What was it, a shag and a chat, some fucking pillow talk?" Steve shouted.

Jacob stood and walked around the room, he'd told her, he told her when they had stayed in the hotel together, but he didn't for the life of him think she would run the story without first telling him. A sickly warm felling rose inside him as he looked at his friend. Steve was still sat bolt upright and forward on the couch. His hands clasped tightly together and his legs twitched up and down.

"I'm sorry, I'll call her, get her to retract it or issue an apology. Get her to say she made it up," Jacob said, trying to calm Steve down.

Steve flopped back and sighed. "It's too late the damage is done, I won't get a job in engineering again, they'll see to that. You know how close the working community is, once it gets known I blabbed, whether or not I did won't matter. I'll be serving up fucking fries at KFC." He sounded beat, and resigned.

Jacob sat down opposite him. "I am sorry."

"It would have come out soon enough anyway," Steve muttered.

"What do you mean?"

Steve looked at him and smiled "Did you get an email to your private server today?"

"That's you? ATMOS?"

"It was. Listen Jacob, if you want to make this up to me, read it and act on it. These engines have altered our magnetosphere somehow; I couldn't conclusively finish my tests in time and so I had to send you what I had in a hurry. That's why I sent it to your private server and marked it a low priority."

"What are they? The effects? Jacob asked.

"Are you still speaking to Alice?"

"I am, I mean I haven't seen her since January but yes, we talk two or three times a week," Jacob answered.

"Read the report, fill in the blanks and get it to her. Maybe if her newspaper prints it NASA would have to act."

"Have to act on what?" Jacob pushed him for an answer.

"You know why we went to Mars. Don't you?" Steve asked.

"Well yeah, to find the origins of life."

"Yeah, for the good of mankind and all that shit." Steve answered sarcastically.

"I'm not following you."

"We went to establish a military platform for long range tactical weapons. You know eventually it won't just

48

be the earth we fight over. There are huge resources in our solar system. That's where the future power lies. Out there."

"That doesn't make sense. If we were going for that why involve the Russians and the Chinese?" Jacob asked.

Steve laughed a little. "The crew of SOL 1 haven't an inkling, they think they're making a leap for mankind, they're as fucking clueless as the dogs the Russians sent up in the fifties as to why they're really there."

Jacob sighed. What if he was right? What if the U.S. Government was using the Martialis mission as a cover? Having information like this was dangerous. A thought occurred to Jacob. "Steve, when did they fire you?"

"A few hours ago, why?" Steve answered.

"And you came straight here?"

"Yes, well no, I went home first and changed and then drove around for a bit. Why does that matter?" Steve asked again, growing concerned.

"No reason, but I'm tired now, I'll look at the report in the morning, you drive safe, go straight home, won't you?"

"Yeah, I need to go to bed anyway, and bring an end to this day," Steve answered.

Jacob walked his friend to the door and stepped out into the cold wet night to watch his friend to his car. As Steve opened the door to climb in Jacob called after him. "Who else have you told about the real reason we're on Mars?"

Steve shook his head. "No one, just you. Why?"

Jacob smiled. "No reason, see you soon."

He watched as Steve backed out of his drive and vanished along the road in a cloud of exhaust fumes and a thickening fog. He closed the door and locked it. Pulling his cell phone from his pocket he pressed the speed dial for Alice. It rang.

Alice answered. "Hi."

"Hey, how are you?"

"I'm good, how are you?" Alice replied.

"I've had Steve David here from NASA, one of the mission specialists, you remember him?" he asked.

"Think I do, short guy, fat with a seventies porn moustache?"

"He got fired today because of an article you ran," Jacob said.

"Oh!" she answered, not seeming to care.

"I told you about the concerns of the propulsion system in confidence. You knew that!"

"I'm sorry, you tell me the engines may cause a problem with our planet, NASA's sitting on it and you want me to keep quiet?" Alice snapped back.

"I thought that seeing as we were half naked and in bed you would have took it as pillow talk."

Alice laughed a little. "That's why I love you, you're so innocent. Are you mad at me? Don't be, I'll do that special thing you like the next time we hook up."

Jacob's anger had left him as soon as he'd heard her voice; he knew deep down whatever he told her would almost always end up in print. He couldn't blame her any more than he could stay mad at her.

"No, I'm not mad. Just be careful next time."

"I will, I promise. Anyway, is it true?"

"Is what true?" Jacob answered.

"Have the engines done something?" Alice pushed for an answer.

"God, you don't give up, do you? I don't know, he's emailed me a report and told me to read it, something to do with our magnetosphere. Anyway, where are you, are you still in London?" he asked changing the subject.

"For now I am, I'm expecting to fly back out to the U.S. to catch up with the Martialis mission after I've covered the European Space Agencies' Encke mission, two weeks, maybe. Why?"

"Oh, no reason, just thinking about that thing you do so well," he said smiling.

"Well, you'll just have to go have a cold shower."

"Guess I will."

Jacob hung up and checked the time, 10:47 p.m. Shaking his head at what had happened tonight he flicked off the lights and went to bed.

10:53 p.m. Local Time: Florida.

373 miles above the earth, the Reuven Ramaty High Energy Solar Spectroscope Imager (RHESSI) spacecraft continued its mission monitoring all of the sun's activity. Launched on February 5th, 2002, it had monitored, taken images and reported back to NASA, countless images of solar flares and Coronal Mass Ejections. In almost every case their impact on how we live and function on earth had typically gone unnoticed. The data came in packets of information, which was then sent to different departments and different individuals within those departments to be analyzed, catalogued, recorded and filed.

RHESSI was sending back routine data. Its spectrometers were pointing toward the sun, searching its surface, looking for signs of flaring or ejections. As one such ejection began its transition, the sun began the first stage of the event as magnetic energy was released along with soft x-ray emissions.

Once detected, the spacecraft deployed its attenuators, designed to protect the delicate instruments on board from being destroyed. But there was a problem. After thirteen years and thousands of movements with perfect operation, giving them results they couldn't have thought of in their wildest dreams, the motors that drove the attenuators over the germanium detectors failed, leaving RHESSI vulnerable. As the second phase started and protons and electrons accelerated to energies exceeding one million electron volts, hard x-rays and gamma rays were emitted, and RHESSI was hit. As it was, it started to fail. When the third and final stage triggered the actual ejection, the instruments that were necessary to the detection and predictions of the sun's activities failed, leaving the spacecraft a dead weight.

In the RHESSI control room, situated in the Goddard Space Flight Center, Greenbelt MD, just outside Washington DC, frantic efforts had begun. With the spacecraft down the sun's surface activity could not be monitored. On duty that evening were Kevin Ricks and Andy Adams. Both men had been with the project now for over three years, and they had the skills and experience to monitor RHESSI as it performed its duties. Tonight, something had gone wrong. For all they knew the artificial crystals which were vital to the imaging systems had been irreparably damaged. Anxiously, they waited as the standard reboot procedure went through its stages, and they also knew that if this didn't work, then they would have to call out the head engineer and team leaders. Whilst for Andy he would see that as a blot on his employment record, Kevin was too laid-back to be concerned over something he had no real control over.

"Come on!" Andy urged the spacecraft back to life. He lived by himself in a small rented apartment in Crofton. He was a neat and tidy man of 23. Particular in everything he did, he would feel responsible for any mishaps.

Kevin sat and watched as the reboot sequence continued. He was different to Andy, he lived in Odenton, and was considered by Andy to be a reprobate, and whilst he was a conscientious worker he had a more laid-back attitude to life. He wouldn't see this in anyway as a reflection on himself. If something had failed on RHESSI, well that wasn't his fault and it wouldn't cause him too much loss of sleep.

"What do we do if this doesn't work?" Kevin asked.

"We have to call the team, you know that." Andy's answer came fast, and with a sharp tone. But his eyes didn't leave the board as he waited to see if the reboot would work. The board lit green just long enough for the monitors to come back life and record the activity. And then the board changed to red, and they knew that RHESSI's working life had come an abrupt end, cut short in its mission because of a group of small motors no bigger than that found in a home printer.

"Shit." Andy repeated as he leaned back in his operators' chair, pushing his hands through his hair.

Kevin picked up the phone, "I'll make the call." The control room quickly became a hive of activity, as everything was tried to save the spacecraft and the mission. But after three hours of running and re-running system checks and restarts, the decision was made, that there was nothing left to do other than bring the spacecraft down in a controlled way, by ditching it into the Atlantic Ocean.

The sun was now in the active phase of its eleven-year cycle, and the suns activity had become more regular and more powerful. One flare during this time could reach temperatures of 100 million degrees, and potentially power the earth for ten million years. But the flares were not the real problem, and they are not what concerned NASA. It was the Coronal Mass Ejections they had to watch during this phase. These ejections carry significantly more material with them and produce shock waves as they travel through interplanetary space. Once they reach earth they often cause geomagnetic storms that can disrupt and destroy high orbit and geostationary satellites. The only good news for the people tasked with observing them, is they take between five to nine days to reach the earth, depending on the size of the shockwave. There was always plenty of warning that such an event would take place. But now with RHESSI down, and the last packet of information still being deciphered, the team had no idea how much power the shock wave carried. All they knew for certain was that it is heading directly for earth.

It was a further two hours before the final data was produced, and this ejection had been huge. Larger than any previously measured, and it had the ability to disrupt mobile phones and GPS, and knock some of the older high orbiting satellites permanently out of action, as well some older transformers on earth causing domestic and industrial power disruptions.

At the speed which they calculated the ejections to be travelling, the shockwave would reach the earth's magnetic field in eight days. At least they had time to issue a general warning and let the public know that they could be inconvenienced for a while. But with RHESSI down, NASA would now need to turn to the European Space Agency, and the four satellites they had monitoring the magnetosphere. That was something that NASA preferred to avoid.

February 21st, 2022. 8.27 a.m. Local Time. Kennedy Space Center.

Jacob had arrived early at work, not so early that it would alert his duty manager, and make for the '*what are you doing in so early?*' conversation, but early enough to ensure he would retrieve the *ATMOS* report from his printer before anyone else would see it. Now he had, and it was packed away in his satchel, his day could start much like any other. He poured a coffee, sat at his desk and began reading the 258-page report he'd printed before he'd received Steve's cryptic message. And whilst it was his intention to at least read it today, Steve's visit last night had spooked him. During the night, what he'd been told about the government using the mission as a cover had grown from a statement made by a disgruntled man who had been fired, to a real concern. He'd decided during a sleepless night he wouldn't share anymore information with Alice, not yet anyway. But what he needed to focus on now was this report. As for Steve's other concern, he would read that at home, away from the office cameras and nosey co-workers.

He'd started reading the file knowing he would be distracted at some point, and ….

It wasn't long before the first of to the day's many distractions landed on his desk. This was one he could do without: Sally was considered, by many, as the office gossip.

"Hi Jacob, how are you doing today?" she asked in her high-pitched voice. Jacob cracked a reluctant smile and turned his head just far enough to make visual contact with her, but avoiding the full eye contact he knew would be a clear signal for Sally to go into full gossip mode.

"I'm okay Sally, thanks. Just snowed under trying to get this report finished and summarized before the boss gets back from his vacation, you know how it is." He replied with enough politeness as not to offend her, but with enough of a tone, that she would pick up on the fact he didn't want to engage with her. But she didn't, and she continued.

"Well it's a shame what happened to those RHESSI boys last night hmm? All that work they've done over there and now, well who knows what?" she babbled out, not knowing herself if she was asking Jacob a question or telling him.

"Yeah, real shame Sally, but I'm sure they'll be okay." Jacob heard little of what she'd just said, he recognized the word RHESSI. There wasn't anyone in the scientific community who didn't know what RHESSI was. But as for the rest, it was all white noise to him. And this time his polite but disinterested approach seemed to work.

"Well, okay Jacob, you keep busy now and I'll see you later." Sally had already left his desk and consciousness by the time she'd finished the end of the sentence.

Jacob tutted a little to himself as she headed away toward the staff lounge. He returned to the report. As he made good progress through it, the thick black hands on the office wall clock swept around its large clear white face, passing the large black numbers as it counted down the end to another work day. Jacob removed his glasses and rubbed his eyes as he squinted at the clock, 3:26 p.m. He stretched and stood making his way for another, and almost certainly eighth, coffee of the day, or was it his ninth? He couldn't remember, and didn't care. Returning to his desk he flicked through the remaining pages, taking care to read the page numbers rather than the text to see how many pages were left, fifty-six to go. It was his final push now to the end, he turned back to the page he'd left his thumb on, and skimmed, looking for anything he would consider of interest.

Almost at the end, a single sentence stopped him dead in its tracks. He leaned into the page, and read the sentence carefully. As he did, he mouthed the words.

"In conclusion, it is clear that the propulsion system used by the SOL 1 spacecraft for the Martialis project, has had an unexpected and profound effect on the earth's magnetic shield, and while it will, over a short time repair itself, it could leave the magnetosphere vulnerable to a solar flare, or coronal mass ejection. As our modern life depends on electricity and satellite communications any weakness in our magnetosphere might cause massive disruption to our way of life with catastrophic consequences. With this in mind I would suggest that all future missions using this technology be launched not from the ground but, from the International Space Station as this would seem to be the safer option."

Jacob paused and read the sentence again, he wanted to be certain he had understood the message, and as he realized he had, he lowered the document down, stood and walked over the where Sally was talking. As he approached he was able to hear the conversation she was having with Emma, a young grad student who had qualified for an intern placement over the winter term. "Emma, I said to her, listen here, I ordered my coffee with separate cream, not with."

Jacob interrupted Sally's rant about the local coffee shop mixing up her order.

"Sally, this morning you mentioned something about RHESSI, what was that?" Jacob asked.

"Well I was telling Emma here about that new coffee shop, and how they always get my order wrong. Why every time I go in that place, they have someone else working the order table, it's no wonder they can't remember the regulars, it wasn't."

Jacob interrupted her again, "Sally what about RHESSI? You said after all of their work, what did you mean by that, has something happened?"

"RHESSI was destroyed last night because its heat shields didn't operate." Sally replied.

"Did they capture any details of the ejection before it went down?" Jacob asked.

"I don't know Jacob, it's only what my brother Andy told me last night. He works over there, called me after it had happened. Woke me up, I told him it was far too late to be calling but he was really upset. He lives alone you know," Sally answered.

Jacob interrupted her again. "Thanks Sally."

As he sat back at his desk, his attention returned to what he'd read and the possible link to the flare that RHESSI had captured before it had failed. He searched the internal NASA intranet for the department and contact numbers. Though RHESSI was based in another department and building, and in fact in another part of the country, the internal extensions were by far the quickest way to get through. He had neither the time nor the inclination to navigate his way around the main switchboard. He dialed and waited for an answer.

"Hello RHESSI control room, Andy Adams speaking." A pleasant voice greeted him.

"Yes, hello." Jacob realized he hadn't prepared any reasonable dialogue for the call he was making. "Yes, hi, my name is Jacob Miller. I'm with the team that's monitoring the Martialis mission."

"Oh hi, yes we know all about that, how are things now? You guys had a little trouble with the comms. I understand. Gave everyone a scare for a while," Andy replied.

"Yes, it's good, just a relay. Listen I'm calling because a work colleague told me you had a problem with the satellite, something about its shields not closing." Jacob asked.

The tone of the voice on the phone changed.

"How do you know that?"

"Your sister, Sally, she told me. But what matters is the data you managed to get before the ejection killed the satellite."

"Why?" was the only reply. Jacob didn't want to start any false alarms; he knew how it would look with his boss, Bruce McCaughey away on vacation. He knew this should go through him, but he also knew that if his assumptions were correct, it couldn't wait until next week.

"Look." Jacob started anxiously but carried on. "I have just read a report on the SOL 1 mission, and more importantly the effects the nuclear fusion rockets had on the earth's magnetic field," Jacob answered.

"Ok, and so?" Andy asked.

Jacob sighed in frustration, but continued, "The report was written by Steve David, he was fired for making this public, well he didn't go to the press with it. Look that doesn't matter, what does matter is that it states it has weakened the field leaving them vulnerable to any large Coronal Ejections should one occur until the shields themselves have regained their strength, so I need to know what knocked out your satellite?"

Jacob listened while he heard a weary sigh come down the line before a voice that whispered with a concerned tone answered him.

"You know where we're based, in the Goddard Space Center?" Andy asked.

"Yes." Jacob confirmed that he did.

"Okay, bring the report here; ask for me, my name is Andy Adams, and Jacob," Andy waited for Jacob to answer.

"Yes Andy?"

"Be as quick as you can." Then the phone clicked. Jacob rested the handset back on to its base, unnerved by the tone of Andy's voice. He looked around the office trying not to let the feelings of imminent doom that swelled and washed around him show on his face. He gathered the report together, collected his jacket and satchel and left the office heading for his parked car.

Jacob sat motionless behind the wheel of his Toyota Camry, clutching at the satchel that now held both reports. Placing it beside on him on the passenger seat he turned the key firing the V6 engine. The built-in satellite navigation system came to life. Jacob programmed in the 870-mile journey that would take him from the Kennedy space center, to Goddard just north of Washington DC. Smiling to himself, he wondered if the oncoming shock wave that was currently hurtling through space would make all of this kind of technology redundant for a while. He had many friends and colleagues who had learned to drive after satnav had become standard in most cars. They'd never developed the skills to read road signs and maps, but then if the only effect was a temporary disruption to things like satnav, TV and cell phones, then he would consider that we had been lucky and escaped with only minor problems. But until he knew what data RHESSI had captured, he couldn't be sure, and that was worth the long dive and stay over, even it meant wearing today's clothes until he returned. Any thoughts of going home first to pack were secondary, and to Jacob, not important. He pushed the cars gear lever into the drive position and pointed the Camry's nose towards the I-95 which would take him through Georgia, South and North Carolina and on toward Washington DC

128 million km above the earth, travelling at 489 kilometers per second, a massive shock wave, one billion tons of space debris and material, travelled toward the earth. And the only person that currently knew of its possible impact on our way of life was racing to bring his

findings and theories to those who may be able to confirm his thesis, and help prevent a catastrophe, the like of which had not been seen by mankind.

Chapter 4
Village Motor Lodge: just off the I-95, near Smithfield

February 22ⁿᵈ, 2022. 3:48 a.m.

Jacob woke with a start, dazed and still half-asleep. The tapping on the window had woken him abruptly. He rubbed his eyes and focused on the figure that stood against the side of his car. Jacob realized it was cop, and now he could see the shadows of blue and red that danced through his car windows. He turned the key and dropped the driver side window.

"Yes officer?" Jacob asked politely.

"You okay son?" the officer asked.

"Yes, I'm on my way to Greenbelt, but I was tired so I pulled over," Jacob explained.

"Then why are you sleeping in your car, in the parking lot of a motel? Why not stay at the motel?" the officer asked.

Jacob thought for a second. "I didn't intend to sleep as long as I have sir, I needed five minutes' rest. But I guess I must have dozed off."

"Well that's as maybe son, but you can't stay here. Either on your way, or it's the motel," the officer said sternly.

Jacob smiled politely. "I can drive now, I'll get going."

Jacob watched as the police officer made his way back to his patrol car. Now awake, he turned the key and rejoined the I-95 toward Green Belt and the Goddard Space Center.

It was a little after 9:00 a.m. when Jacob pulled his Camry up to the main gate at Goddard. The security guard walked out of the small hut and leant against his car. Jacob dropped the window.

"I'm here to see Andy Adams," Jacob announced.

"Is he expecting you?"

"Tell him Jacob Miller is here from Kennedy, he'll know who I am," Jacob replied

The guard returned to his hut and Jacob watched as he picked up the phone and began talking. After a few minutes of talking and the guard staring out at Jacob he put the phone down and waved him through as the barrier lifted. Jacob followed the road through and then turned to follow the signs that read RHESSI He reached a small parking lot and stopped. As he did a small grey door opened in the corner of the building opposite him and a slim neatly dressed man walked out and toward him. Jacob switched off the engine and climbed out locking the car as he did.

"Jacob Miller?" The man said as he approached.

"Yes," Jacob answered.

By now he had reached Jacob and had held out his hand. "Andy Adams." Jacob took his hand and shook it.

"It's nice to finally be here."

"How was the drive?" Andy asked.

"Long, I fell asleep somewhere and was woken up by a cop banging on my window."

"Well you're here now." Andy pointed back to the steel door he'd emerged from.

Jacob followed him into the building and along a corridor into the RHESSI control room. Sat at one of the many terminals was a man in what Jacob thought was his mid-twenties but not as tidy or well dressed as Andy. His hair was unkempt, and his jeans and t-shirt had obviously passed the date they should have been washed.

"This is Kevin; he works with me here," Andy introduced him.

Jacob reached across and shook hands. "Nice to meet you."

"And you too. Andy says you have concerns over RHESSI going down, and SOL 1?"

Jacob turned to Andy. "Who else did you tell?"

Andy squirmed a little. "No one else, just Kevin, we thought we'd hear what you had to say before we did anything."

Jacob sighed. "Then we'd better get started."

February 22nd, 2022. 2:27 p.m. GMT, House of Commons: London, United Kingdom.

Alice sat in her assigned seat, listening to yet another statement by yet another government minister trying once again to save the career of his Prime Minister. The scandal had started two days previous and Alice had been hastily assigned to cover it much against her wishes, because the journalist who would normally cover political events was at the NATO summit on I.S. Alice had started as a political reporter but moved over to become the papers science reporter after she'd had to take time off because of Rob's illness. Sitting here reminded her of how much she preferred her normal job. She had seen three Prime Ministers come and go along with a multitude of faceless and forgettable ministers. And yet here she was again listening to an explanation of the latest government gaff.

Because of her previous experience as the political journalist, Alice's editors had decided she would better serve the paper by using her tenacious energy and drive getting to the bottom of what could be the worst speech a British PM had made since the 'peace in our time' speech, made by Neville Chamberlain in 1938. But Alice was frustrated. She was frustrated at not being the U.S. and not seeing Jacob. The speech seemed to drone on endlessly, and Alice found herself becoming immune to rhetoric, and sound bites that seemed to spew from the PM's with almost automatous repetition.

But as with all things, even good things, it ended, and Alice could escape. Even though outside it was cold, and raining, it was better than staying here any longer than she needed too. As she made her way toward the taxi line, her phone vibrated in her jacket pocket. She looked at the screen and smiled warmly when she saw the name Jacob. Retreating into the shelter of the taxi stand she pressed the answer button.

"Hi Jacob, how are you? Have you heard from Steve again?"

"Are you coming back to the U.S. soon?" his tone was short, and with worry.

"Not yet, I'm being forced to cover Westminster, so I'm in miserable London. It's cold and dark. Why?"

"Listen closely. I'm not going into detail over the phone, but you need to get to Washington DC as soon as you can. Do you understand?"

Alice's mood and manner changed. "I'll need more than that if I want my boss to fly me to Washington."

"Sorry Alice, I can't give you more than that." Jacob sighed wearily and continued, "I've been here two days. I drove nine hours to get here. Believe me this is big. You need to be here!"

"I'll see what I can do. Where are you?" she asked him. Her investigative instincts were still working in the background of her consciousness.

"I can't tell you that on the phone, just get to Dulles International. I'll meet you there," he whispered.

"Then where are we going?" Alice didn't get to finish the question. Jacob's phone cut off.

Placing her phone back into her pocket she climbed into the back of a black cab and entrusted its driver to take her to her newspapers offices in Fleet Street. She knew this was serious, she knew that she had to convince Mike of another trip to the U.S. and another long stay over. But she did not understand what she was trying to convince him of, and she couldn't let him know how much she trusted Jacob. Like Alice, Mike had a keen nose for stories and if she made the trust and relationship with Jacob sound too obvious, she knew he would be able to figure out what she felt about him, and news like that doesn't stay private for long.

She entered Mike's office and sat opposite him, smiling. Mike looked up from behind his desk, over his half-size glasses. "What is it?"

"I need to go back to the States."

"You've got to be kidding me, you're there more than Branson," Mike replied sharply.

"I've got a lead from my contact at NASA, something about the Martialis mission," she said, bluffing her way through.

"What is it?" he asked.

"I don't know the specifics. All I know is it could be big."

"You know this story about the PM's speech is going to run. And with Stewart away covering I.S I need you here."

"I.S will still be fighting when I get back. That's if Putin hasn't blown them all to hell, or wherever they reckon they go." Alice pleaded.

Mike sighed and took off his glasses, wiping them with his handkerchief. "What about Encke?"

"You know this press conference is only to be an update on the mission. Send an intern, they'll love it."

"Two weeks, there and back. If you haven't got a story by then you come home."

Alice smiled at him. "I will, I'll have a story for you. Thanks."

Alice left his office and sat at her desk in the newsroom, and booked the flight. She knew convincing Mike was the easy part. Her and Rob had made plans to spend this weekend with their children at their former family home where Rob and the children still lived. Rob had made it clear since they'd separated, that he wanted to try again with their marriage. Alice knew it wouldn't work, but if she flat-out told him this, she'd also have to tell him about Jacob, and Alice wasn't sure Rob could handle that on top of their separation. And she had her two sons to think of. So reluctantly she'd agreed to this weekend on the condition they slept in separate rooms, which Rob had agreed to. After all, he'd gone to a lot of trouble to make it go well. Alice sat in the back of the cab going over in her mind what she would say to Rob. There were days back when they were together that the journey from her office to their home seemed to take an age. But as Alice battled to think of way to break the news that she would not be staying, today's journey seemed to come to an end far too quickly.

As she entered their home she could tell Rob was trying. The smell of fresh coffee and bread wafted through the hall, and in the background the album they'd listened to while courting was playing, Rob took her coat and bags and placed them down before giving her a hug. Alice reciprocated but only in the same way she hugged a friend. Before she explained to Rob what the change of plans would be, he had already spotted that the taxi had not left.

"You're not staying, are you?" Rob asked.

Alice shook her head. "I have to go back to the States; something has come up."

"America! Again?" Rob shouted as Alice told him about the change of plans.

"Yes Rob, I'm the U.S. correspondent, you remember that, don't you? Alice shouted back.

"Of course I remember that, you won't let me bloody forget it, will you?"

"Oh, grow up Rob. Okay, you got sick, okay our lives haven't turned out as we planned them, but deal with it, just fucking deal with it and fucking live with it!" Alice's shouting stopped and her tone became softer. "That's what I do, every bloody day. I just live with it."

Rob's aggressive stance slumped and his shoulders sagged, he looked at her with an expression of pity on his face. Not for her. The pity that was written across his face was for him, it even wrapped itself around his spoken words.

"That's what you do, you just deal with it? That's what our life together meant for you, just dealing with each day until you got the chance to escape to America again?" he said softly.

He watched her head for the door, she turned around and smiled softly, as if she was both saddened and pleased that she'd blurted out how she really felt.

"Look Rob, the taxi is waiting. I'll be back in about a week or so and then I promise I'll stay for the weekend. For the boys."

"I love you, you know." Rob spoke gently as she disappeared through the door, but Alice didn't reply.

He watched from the window as she climbed into the cab, hoping she would look back, but Alice didn't. She slammed the car door and in a plume of condensation from the tail pipe, Alice and the car vanished.

Rob heard the living room door squeak open, he turned to see Ben and Max emerge, and Rob's heart sank. How much of that did they hear? He did his best to reassure them and change the moment.

"Hey, you two, how are my big lads?" he said, smiling.

As usual it was Ben that spoke for them both. "Is mummy coming back daddy?"

Rob tried hard to fight back the emotion that had swollen up inside him, and with a half-cocked smile he headed toward them holding out a guiding hand.

"Of course Mummy's coming back. You know how her work can be. She's off on important business. Now who wants fish and chips for tea?" Rob asked the boys.

They soon forgot about the conversation they'd heard between their mom and dad as the thought of a walk down to the local village fish and chip shop and the promise of what that held quickly achieved what Rob hoped it would. A distraction.

February 23rd, 2022. 10:37 a.m. Local Time. Dulles Airport, Washington DC.

The flight to Washington was a mixture of reading in-flight magazines, trying to sleep and watching, or at least semi watching, a movie on the tiny screen in front of her. As the American Air Cruisers flight touched down at Dulles International, and Alice was once again making her way through the crowds of other people, embracing their own *meeter's and greeters,* made up of the usual families and friends, Alice caught sight of Jacob. But unlike all of the other times they'd met up he looked disheveled and exhausted.

Her feeling of teenage giddiness and excitement soon fell away when she saw him. Nevertheless, she raised her usual smile and walked toward him, opening her arms as she got closer in readiness to give him his customary hug, after which she pulled away still holding onto his arms and smiled.

"Hi, it's good to be back here and with you." Alice spoke softly and lovingly, as she kept contact with him.

"It's good to see you too, but you must think I'm a complete mess," he answered, aware of how he looked.

Alice smiled and released her grip on him.

"Well I wondered if this was some new look that hadn't made its way over the pond yet?"

Jacob shook his head, still wearing an ever-decreasing smile.

"No, this is the not showering or resting for 3 days look."

"It must be important then?" Alice replied.

"You have no idea. Come on, I need to get back and you have to see this.

"Tell me now; I've been trying to guess what this big story is. I hope you haven't brought me here over this propulsion thing again?" Alice asked.

"I'll explain soon. It's not far."

Jacob led Alice outside to his waiting Camry. He put her bags in the trunk. Once they were both in the car, he turned the key and headed back to RHESSI control in Goddard. It was a short drive and though Alice tried to make her customary small talk, she could tell by Jacob's lack of replies and interest he had too much on in his mind, and so a little over half way she abandoned her attempts, and instead turned to watch the scenery pass by the window.

As they approached the Goddard Space Flight Center Jacob spoke for the first time since they'd gotten into the car.

"Okay Alice, what you're about to hear is so far only known by three people. Me, Kevin Ricks and Andy Adams, and no one else. Do you understand? No one."

Alice nodded. She heard the solemnity in his voice, and she knew he was speaking partly out of authority and partly, and rather worryingly now, out of fear.

"I promise Jacob, it won't go any further," Alice assured him.

They approached the main gate. The guard recognized Jacob and waved them through. Alice noticed a black leather pouch hanging from his side, the handle of an automatic pistol was visible.

Once parked, Jacob turned to face Alice.

"Follow me and I'll take you in."

Alice followed Jacob through the security doors and into the darkened control room, the bank of monitors and control systems provided most the light. Sat by what Alice assumed was the main control area was two men. Alice noticed immediately that both men had a solemn and somewhat grave expression on their faces. Jacob turned to Alice.

"This is Andy and Kevin, the two I mentioned earlier. Guys this is Alice."

They took it in turns to say hello and then sat down. Jacob made sure the door was secured and then turned to Alice.

"Okay, what I'm about to tell you no one else knows yet."

"Yet?" Alice asked with a confused tone.

Jacob nodded. "A few days ago, I received a report from Steve that detailed the launch of SOL 1, and it referred to an effect the engines had on the earth's magnetic shielding, the magnetosphere. At the same time RHESSI monitored a large coronal mass ejection from the sun, but before it could gather its normal level of information a malfunction left the imaging systems vulnerable, and it was destroyed."

"Why do I get the idea this will not be good guys?" Alice asked.

"Just before I called you yesterday we managed to salvage some of the information that RHESSI had been able to obtain. We put it together with the data we received from the European Space Agency's satellites that monitor the sun, and we're just waiting for the computer to finish the ejection model based on that data."

Alice folded her arms in frustration. "I hope you haven't brought me across to the U.S. for nothing more than story about a failed satellite."

Jacob sighed and explained it again, but before the first words left his mouth, Andy cut across him.

"Don't you get it? The sun erupted on a massive scale; we've never measured anything this big before."

"Yes, I get that, I am a scientific reporter and I know that solar flares and eruptions happen all the time." Alice interrupted Andy.

"This wasn't a solar flare. It was a coronal mass ejection. One of the most violent, and destructive forces in the universe," Andy replied.

Alice turned back to Jacob. "Okay so that's the science, what's the story?"

Jacob turned and nodded to Andy as if to signify that he could handle her questions from this point on.

"The story is this. Because of the impact that SOL 1 had on the magnetosphere, and the just shit bad timing of this ejection, we expect that most of the communication and GPS satellites will be wrecked, and that some of the older power stations will be overloaded. And that all over the world we will be able see an aurora," Jacob answered.

Alice looked between the three of them.

"When?"

"Within the next twenty-four to thirty-six hours. We think," Andy said.

"You think?" Alice questioned him.

"Although light from the sun reaches us in around nine minutes, an ejection usually takes around nine days to reach the earth, but with RHESSI down we can't predict its speed, so it's our best guess," Jacob answered.

Alice turned back to Jacob, "You said so far?"

"What?" Jacob asked, puzzled.

"You said you're waiting for the computer to finish modelling the ejection. How long until we have that?"

Jacob turned to Andy and Kevin and shrugged. This time Kevin answered.

"Anytime. It's only because the system must fill in so many blanks this its taking this long, I expect that within the next hour we will have an accurate model, or at least as accurate as this can be with the limited data we have."

"You said earlier you had data from the European Space Agency," Alice said.

"We do, but their satellites aren't as detailed as RHESSI, so we still need to fill in the blanks," Andy answered.

Alice looked back at Jacob. "Let me get this straight, you've flown me across the Atlantic because some people will have to read a map rather than rely on a satnav. Are you trying to piss me off?" she snapped.

Jacob showed the patience and wit that had first attracted Alice to him. "It's more than that. Once we have the completed model, whatever it says must be reported to the department heads, who will show it to theirs and so on, until someone way up the ladder will file it and say nothing. But now you know about it you can write it up, and warn people that their power may go off, that their cell phones will stop working, and they'll lose their internet connection as well cable and satellite TV. This will be big for you, and it will validate the story you ran on the propulsion system of SOL 1," Jacob explained.

Alice wasn't convinced. A few inconveniences because of something she assumed most people would neither see nor feel the effects of, wasn't as a big a story as Jacob was making it to be. She wondered if it was a vain attempt by Jacob to get her over here, or to absolve Steve David. But she dismissed that thought as quickly as it had come to mind. His appearance wasn't that of man trying to make a good impression, and on the drive from the airport when the conversation would normally turn to plans of passion, he had been distant, not just from Alice, but almost everything. He seemed only focused on getting here.

She watched him closely as Andy signaled him over to where he and Kevin sat. The three of them huddled, looking over what she assumed was the final model they had been waiting for. But something was wrong. Kevin had a look of dread on his face. He had turned an ashen white, and it looked to Alice that he would vomit at any moment, and as she kept watching Kevin he reached for the square metal bin next to his desk and emptied the contents of his stomach into it. Alice became concerned.

Andy looked no better than Kevin. He now had the same startled and frightening look on his face. Kevin rose from his seat and without saying a word he headed away from the console and out into the small corridor. Andy and Jacob spoke in hushed whispers and Jacob became agitated.

His body language gave away his ever-increasing uneasiness, even though he'd maintained his whispers.

Alice started over to Andy and Jacob, from behind Jacob's body Alice noticed Andy spy her as she moved toward them both, and in the same way a guilty man would when facing his accuser, he dropped his head and placed it in his hands, but it was what he did next that made Alice stop in her tracks.

"Jacob?" Alice whispered in an apprehensive tone.

Jacob turned around to face her. He had the same ashen and gaunt look that Kevin had only moments before he had vomited.

"Jacob what is it?" she whispered again.

Jacob turned and looked once more at Andy and nodded to him. Andy nodded in return, and then Jacob turned back to Alice, the color returned to his face and as it did his expression turned from one of dismay to one of panic. He cleared his throat.

"We have to go now, you can't be here, I'll explain in the car." He turned back to Andy and continued, "You'll give us an hour yes?"

Andy nodded.

Jacob turned back to Alice grabbing her forearm, he looked straight at her. "We have to go. Now!"

Alice didn't struggle, she didn't resist. Something in her had always trusted him and now it seemed to her for reasons she couldn't explain to herself, that she should trust him again.

Whatever this was, whatever had changed in those few moments when they'd huddled around the desk meant that she was no longer supposed to be here, and Jacob was leading her to safety. They left the building and sat in Jacobs's car, she watched him as he backed out of the parking bay. Jacob looked nervous, not as cool and collected as he'd looked when they had arrived a short time ago.

As he approached the gate the guard smiled and raised it for them. Seeing that the road was clear Jacob planted his foot down hard on the accelerator and the engine revved.

As it did, the front of the car raised as the speedometer rose rapidly, passing the speed limit. Jacob had never driven so fast, he adored this car because it had once belonged to his father.

"Jacob, slow down, you're frightening me. What's wrong? What's happened?" she asked

"I can't slow down. I have to get you back to the airport and then you need to go back. Catch the first plane home, do you hear me, don't leave the airport. Go through passport control and stay there until your flight is called. Trust me Alice." He replied with a sharp tone.

"What is it?" Alice continued with her questioning, but Jacob stayed defiant.

"I can't tell you, for your own sake you weren't here, fly home, and wait for me to contact you," he said

"What? Jacob you're not making any sense." Did she want to know what had changed, or should she go home and forget about it? She couldn't, that's why she did what she did. She dug and scraped for stories that no one else would see. "What the fuck is going on?" she asked again.

A noise made them both jump, and the tension in the car now was tangible. The bleep came again. Jacob realized with relief it was his phone. It was Andy.

"Jacob, don't go to the airport. Kevin's told them, they know you were here; they've put an APB out for you both. They want us all together. They want to debrief us."

Alice watched as once again Jacobs's expression changed. He lowered his window and threw his phone out of the car and then he slammed on the brakes and brought the Camry to a dead stop. He turned to Alice, tears once again swelling up in his eyes.

"I'm sorry for bringing you over, for involving you."

Chapter 5
Baltimore-Washington Highway

February 23rd, 2022. 4:27 p.m. EST.

As Jacob continued his apology, he pushed down on the small red clip that held Alice's seatbelt buckle, it released and Jacob reached across and opened her door.

"It's best you get out Alice."

Alice was in shock. "What the fuck are you talking about, I'm not getting out, what is happening Jacob?"

Jacob pointed over Alice's shoulder "That road is Riverdale Road. Follow it until the intersection with Annapolis Road, take a left, there you'll see a motel called the Metro Points Motel. Stay there until I call you. Oh, and Alice, dump your cell phone."

Alice looked back at Jacob and then to the road he was pointing at. The panic she had pushed down was now building back up. She didn't know what to do. She did not understand what she was now involved in, and she could tell by the alarm that now washed over Jacob's face, that this was no longer about a few satnavs and cell phones not working. As her mind scrambled, Jacob repeated his instruction, but this time he was yelling them, and the sudden aggression his voice brought her thoughts back to the moment.

"Alice go now!" Jacob shouted at her.

But it was too late. As Alice stepped out of the Camry, two large black SUV's with blue and red flashing lights pulled up alongside them and Alice knew her time to escape and follow Jacobs instructions had come and gone. She slumped back into her seat as the two front doors of the lead SUV opened, and two men wearing black suits walked over to them. The tallest of the men walked to Jacob's side, whilst the second man stood directly in front of the Camry. Jacob lowered his window and the man lowered himself down to talk to him. "Jacob Miller?"

Jacob answered nervously. "Yes."

"Pull your car over to the side sir, and come with me," the tall man said.

Jacob nodded and signaled Alice to close her door. The two men watched as Jacob pulled the Camry off the road and onto the grass embankment opposite the Parkdale High School. Jacob switched off the engine and turned to Alice.

He leant over to Alice and whispered. "Just do what they say, and remember I haven't told you much."

Alice glared back at him. "What have you involved me in Jacob?"

Jacob's expression was sad again. "I'm sorry Alice. When I called, you we had no idea it would be this bad."

"What would be this bad? Jacob what is it?" Alice felt scared.

But Jacob didn't answer. The doors of the car were opened by the suited men and Jacob and Alice knew it was time to join them in their ominous looking SUV's. The larger of the two men took the keys from the Camry's ignition and pressed the lock button, as he did he turned to Jacob. "Don't worry, you'll get them back."

Placed in different vehicles Jacob and Alice were driven back to the Goddard Space Center. They were led from the car park and into what Alice thought looked like a meeting room. It was a long room with a central table, with standard office chairs and furniture placed neatly around it. A white screen hung down the far wall and a ceiling mounted projector hovered above the table.

"Wait here." The larger man left the room closing the door behind him.

Alice sat in the first chair she reached. Her knees felt weak and adrenaline pumped through her body. What was she in the middle of? What had Jacob gotten her involved in? She had to know, if she was to be treated this way, with the suspicion that she'd seen in the men's eyes then she had a right, Christ, she deserved to know what Jacob, Andy and Kevin had been so frightened by. Jacob sat in the adjacent chair. Clasping his hands together, he lowered his head. He was visibly shaken and scared. Alice reached across with one hand and tentatively placed it over his clasped hands.

"What is it?" she asked.

"It's best you don't know Alice. That way you're not implicated," he answered.

"I think it's too late for that Jacob. I'm here with you, and I've been locked in this room by your government's goons, and now you're telling me it's best I don't know. Tell me now," she demanded.

Jacob raised his head and sighed. "The model that came back wasn't what we had expected it to be. We thought the coming shockwave and debris from the ejection would knock a few satellites out, maybe disrupt a few power supplies that depend on the older electricity stations that aren't shielded against an EMP. But it's much worse, far worse than either myself, Andy or Kevin had thought it might be."

Alice moved her position to be closer to him. "An Electromagnetic Pulse?" she confirmed.

"Yes, and this one might be as powerful as the one caused by the Hiroshima atomic bomb, anything electrical not hardened against it will fry, rendering it useless," Jacob confirmed.

"What type of things?" she asked.

"Everything that requires a microchip or circuit board, and these days that's everything from your electric toothbrush, to your car and home computer. Everything we depend on today uses some sort of microchip. Telecommunications will go out; aircraft will stop mid-flight, trains, ships, cars, the banking system, TV and radio. In the snap of a finger we will be back in the stone age."

"But the government has a plan to deal with these things. How long would it take to get things working again?" Alice replied.

Jacob laughed a little and looked back toward Alice. "Working again? You don't get it. Your phone will be useless. It can't be repaired, nor can the computer networks, or any effected technology. It will all have to be replaced. Worldwide, every device, everything we use or don't even know we use. Debit and credit cards will cease to work. When people become unable to draw cash from their accounts, can you imagine what will be next? No water or heating. Nothing, do you get it? Nothing will work."

Alice sat back in her chair, pulling her comforting hand away from Jacob and placing it to her mouth. "Why do they want us back here?" she asked, more out of the need to keep focused than the need to hear the answer.

"Because it's worse than that." Jacob looked back down and paused before he continued. "You've watched Star Trek, yes?"

"Hasn't everyone?" Alice replied.

"Well the shields that protect the earth, the magnetosphere, work much like the shields of the Enterprise. That's where they got the idea for the show, but when the Klingons hit them with enough fire power they collapsed right?"

"Yeah okay, so?"

"When SOL 1 left the earth it damaged and weakened the magnetosphere as it passed through it, not by much, and in time it would have repaired itself, but this ejection from the Sun is the largest ever recorded. The model we ran has identified a part of the shield above the South Pole that will collapse when the shock wave hits. Without an intact magnetic shield, our atmosphere is vulnerable to the things that make space a lethal place to be," Jacob explained.

Alice understood now what had made Kevin vomit, and what had made Andy and Jacob act the way they had. As she sat in silence, Jacob continued with the details. "The International Space Station, the ISS, is in a low orbit and is protected by the magnetosphere. It protects the astronauts from the lethal radiations of space, but when this hits, they will have no protection and we don't have the time to rescue them."

Alice turned back to Jacob. "What? You mean they'll be left to just die up there?"

"There is nothing anybody can do? We just don't have the time," Jacob replied.

"But there must be some warning systems to prevent this?" Alice asked.

"There is, I mean was," Jacob said. "It was RHESSI."

"What about the crew of SOL 1. They're on Mars. They must be told. You have to get a message to them. Jacob this is your department, you have to convince them," Alice demanded.

As Alice finished speaking, the door opened and Andy and Kevin entered followed by the large man and four other individuals. Two were agents they hadn't yet been introduced to, and the other two Jacob knew. It was his boss Bruce McCaughey, the head of the Martialis mission, and the head of RHESSI, Andy and Kevin's boss, Michael Forbes. Each of them took their place around the table and sat in silence. First to speak was the large man that had brought them back to the center.

"For those who don't know my name, I'm special agent Burton with the FBI. I'm here because Kevin informed Mr Forbes of the potential problems we may face when the coming shockwave impacts with the earth, which I understand is expected in the next twenty-four to thirty-six hours. The thing is this; we don't need or want any unnecessary public panicking. We have protocols in place for such events, and it is better to keep the public unaware of what they need not know. If the President requests it we can try and make sure that air traffic and other vulnerable technology that would cause the loss of life if it was to be affected by this are out of service, but without a definite event time, it will be almost impossible. On that basis, it has been agreed that you will all stay here as our guests, and that you will hand over all cell phones and other devices you can use to contact people until the event has passed."

Alice was the first to react, her natural detestation of all things oppressive rising to the surface.

"So you're keeping us here against our will. Well I for one am not staying. I have a family and home to get back to." Alice started to stand but agent Burton moved so close to her she had no room to maneuver out of the chair. He looked down on her, smiled and spoke.

"Sorry Ma'am but it would be best if you were to stay with the rest."

Alice protested. "I'm a British citizen. What you're doing is illegal; you cannot hold people against their will with no good reason!"

"Actually, Ms Fisher, I think you will find I can and that I am. Just until the event is over you understand, then you'll be free to go on your way."

Agent Burton then turned to Bruce McCaughey and Michael Forbes. "Will you two gentlemen come with me? You have an appointment with the President."

As agent Burton opened the door, the two other agents that had come in with him made their way around to stand by it. He introduced them.

"This is Agent Anderson and Special Agent Frakes. They'll be looking after you while you stay here. Oh, and Mr Miller, I've been told your car is back here. Agent

Frakes will keep the keys safe until you can leave." With that he smiled and left the room, closing the door behind him.

Alice, Jacob, Kevin and Andy sat in silence. No one wanted to be the first to speak. Agent Anderson was the first to break the uncomfortable and somewhat tangible silence. "Agent Frakes and I will be just outside the door." With that the two men left the room.

Jacob spoke first. "Jesus Kevin what the fuck did you do that for? We agreed one hour before we would say anything. Give Alice a chance to get a flight home and for me to be on my way."

Kevin looked awkward. "I panicked ok? I had just seen a model forecast that will change this world forever and I freaked out okay? Fuck! You think I wanted to tell anyone or even see that shit!"

Andy was the first to reply, "We all freaked out Kevin, but dragging Jacob and Alice back into this won't help anybody, will it? What do you think they'll do next?"

"What do you mean next?" Alice asked with a concerned tone, "They said we can go once the event had passed."

Andy laughed, "You believe that shit? You believe anything a U.S. Government agent says? Shit, you Brits really are fucking naïve."

"What the fuck is that supposed to mean?" she snapped back.

"It means there is no after the event. The Aurora will be seen worldwide, and that's just the beginning, that's just the shockwave impacting on the magnetosphere. The shit that happens next will be the main event, once everything is fucked there will be no after the event, we will be right in the middle of the event."

The room fell silent again.

Alice spoke first. "Is there any chance this EMP won't happen? I mean what if it doesn't or it's not as big as you first thought it could be. Wouldn't everything then go on as normal?"

Kevin answered, "There is a small chance that it won't be as bad as the model predicted, but we don't know because there is no bench mark for these things, no independent validating, so we have to use the IB, *err* the isotropy boundary. This measures the precipitation of energetic particles measured by the polar spacecraft. We observe them at ionospheric altitudes. By using hundreds of theses IB observations we can model this as well, if not better than using the solar-wind based models. For this prediction, we used the standard T96 or Tsyganenko 1995 because we can compare the magnetic field at specific points inside the magnetosphere, this means..."

Alice cut him off. "In English, anyone?"

Jacob took over, "The models are quite accurate, but they are only models based on the information we have at any one time. A change in the solar winds can affect the outcomes and where they may happen, but the fact remains that with an ejection this size and an already weakened magnetic field, something will happen."

"But, it could be less than you think?" Alice looked for a positive, anything that she felt might bring some optimism back to the day.

"Yes, but it could be a lot worse," Andy replied.

The mood in the room dropped, and again it fell silent. The time seemed to drag by. Alice was convinced that the clock was running backward when none of them were watching it just to make the day longer. Andy and Kevin had both long since adopted the sleeping position of bored teenagers, laying their heads on their folded arms atop the desk. Jacob too had succumbed to the boredom and tedium that this grey walled, faceless and uninspiring meeting room oozed. With his head bent back over the chair and his legs stretched out he was snoring. She smiled as his chest rose and fell. But Alice felt trapped, alone, and vulnerable.

She must have dozed off herself, because she awoke with a start, confused and dry mouthed when the door had been opened and closed. Agent Burton came into view along with Bruce McCaughey and Michael Forbes. Alice looked up at the clock; it was now 10:27 p.m. She didn't remember falling asleep, but the fact was she had, they all had, and by the look on the faces of Andy, Kevin and Jacob they'd been woken by the same door slamming.

Once again, the door was closed and the six of them were left alone. Jacob was the first to stand and stretch. He made his way around the table and to his boss Bruce, holding out his hand, offering a welcome.

"Hi Bruce. How did it go with the President?"

Bruce shook his outstretched hand and replied with a question, the one Jacob knew was coming. "Never mind that, why' you here and what is that journalist doing here? Bruce asked.

Jacob took a deep breath. "When I learned of RHESSI's problems, I called the control room because of the report I'd read regarding the effects SOL 1 had on the earth's magnetic fields."

"Which report? I hadn't seen any report on this subject," Bruce asked.

"It was sent to my private email by Steve David and was classified as low importance so the server's security wouldn't pick it up," Jacob answered.

"Him again, he's already caused us enough embarrassment going public with that," Bruce said.

Jacob knew now he'd have to come clean about Steve. "Bruce, Steve didn't leak that, I did, but by accident."

Bruce glared at him. "What do you mean by accident?" he snapped.

Alice spoke before Jacob answered. "It was me, Jacob told me in confidence, and I ran the story."

"And yet here you are!" Bruce said, before turning on Jacob. "And you, when this is over you're fired along with your friend Steve."

At this moment, Jacob didn't care about his job, and had been expecting Bruce to fire him once he knew who really leaked the information. "Bruce listen, Steve was right. The engines did weaken our magnetosphere; they are partly to blame for what is coming."

Bruce sat and sighed. "Don't you think we know that?

"And yet you went ahead with the launch?" Alice asked.

"Yes, because the shields would have repaired, over time, a few months perhaps, but they would have repaired themselves. This is just bad timing."

"Bad fucking timing?" Alice snapped.

Jacob signaled to Alice to calm down. "Look, this is where we're at. Blaming each other won't change that, but we have a chance to warn people, to make preparations."

"You have. Right? That's why you went to see the President, to tell him so he can warn people, get FEMA on stand-by," Andy, asked Michael.

Michael answered with a sigh, "We didn't see the President; we saw his scientific aid and briefed him on what we think the shockwave from the ejection will do. And they're in contact with the ISS, they're using their own instruments to monitor it."

"What preparations are they making? Are they grounding air traffic until the event has passed?"

Michael shook his head. "Nothing like that. We had a look at the model you produced, and to be honest we think you've over exaggerated the results, and the ISS confirms it won't be as big as you've conjected it will be. Besides there have been ejections similar to these in the past and they've caused nothing but minor disruption."

Andy stood. "You must be kidding. You know this shockwave is massive. We've seen nothing like this before. How could you possibly think that the model is inaccurate? There are people who will die. People on planes, ships, in cars and what about the ISS? You know their equipment isn't as accurate as RHESSI was, or even the European satellites and what about their safety? Did you mention that to the scientific adviser while you were covering your own fucking ass?"

Bruce walked around the table. He reached the head of the table and assumed a position he was more used to, more comfortable in and then addressed them all with his polished delivery.

"Listen, we don't know what effect this shockwave will have, if it will indeed have any effect. We are in uncharted waters here. We estimate the shockwave will hit our planet at ten-thirty local time. tomorrow morning and that the southern Polar Regions will be worst hit, assuming that the prevailing solar winds stay as they are. And according to the information the White House has, and from what Commander Relford on board the ISS has said, it looks like they will."

"That's too early." Alice turned to Jacob. "You said the next twenty-four to thirty-six hours."

Bruce continued, taking great delight in what he said next. "Something else you seemed to have got wrong Jacob?" Jacob glared at Bruce but he continued. "We expect the auroras will be seen by around eighty-five percent of the world and that the geomagnetic storm itself will last no more than four hours. The President is informing governments around the world of the impending light show, but that's all it will be. Nature giving us a great show."

Andy spoke up, "You know as well as I do that the four hours is only the geomagnetic phase. That doesn't take into account the SSC, or the recovery phase."

Alice cut in. "What's that?"

Andy turned to her. "A storm like this normally consists of three elements, the SSC, or the storm sudden commencement, the main phase of the storm and then the recovery phase. This is when the magnetosphere recovers and it can take up to seven days."

Bruce interrupted Alice's physics lesson. "Yes Andrew, but you know that not all storms have three phases, don't you?"

"That's true, but this storm is unlike anything we've measured before, and you know that. Don't you?"

Kevin was the next to speak up. "Michael what strength rating did you predict the storm to be?"

Michael shifted in his seat, "We told the White House we're expecting an intense storm of around -50nT to -200nT," he answered.

"What?" Kevin was clearly agitated by Michael's answer. "You know as well as the rest of us do in this room that this storm will not be an intense storm."

"That's a good thing then, right?" Alice asked.

"No!" Kevin spun around and sighed before he answered. "This is going to be much worse, and he fucking knows it." Kevin's voice was now strained and Alice could tell that this was a voice that was not used to conflict and shouting, but Kevin carried on.

"All the model results pointed to a storm much bigger, something closer to a ....

Super-storm event, or even greater, measuring up toward -650nT."

Bruce leaped to Michael's defense. "We haven't seen a storm that strong since we started recording these events. You're just scare mongering, trying to make a name for yourselves."

"You honestly think that's what this is about, getting our name in some journal or magazine. What would be the point? When we're back in the fucking stone-age who's gonna read it?" Jacob answered and continued, but with a calmer tone. "Listen, Bruce, you've seen the data, you know what the model predicted, and even if the prediction is out, you know it's going be much worse than you've told the White House." But his calmer friendlier approach didn't alter Bruce and Michael's stance, and with one sweeping comment from Michael the room once again fell in to silence.

"Well, we'll see in a few hours, until then I suggest we all just shut the hell up."

Alice pulled Jacob to one side; she needed to ask him another question about the conversation, not for her journalistic tendencies, but for herself. She was worried that by asking too many questions in the open she would lose even more respect and status than she already had. And that was assuming that she had any left.

"Jacob what do they mean by -650nT?"

"A geomagnetic storm is measured in disturbance equals storm equals time, or DST for short. We measure the average global change in the earth's horizontal magnetic field at the magnetic equator. And, because we have an array of magnetometer stations, we can measure it in just about real time."

"But what is an nT?"

"A Tesla is a measurement of a magnetic field, a Nano Tesla or nT is just a smaller measurement of a Tesla, the higher the negative the worse it is, so an event measuring -650nT is much worse than one measuring 550nT."

"Yes, I remember that from college. But what would this storm mean for us?" Alice asked.

"But here's the thing. In 1989, a severe geometric storm caused the collapse of the Hydro-Québec power grid in seconds, over six million people were left with no power for nearly nine hours, and that storms DST was measured at -589nT. Imagine a storm much more powerful, hitting an already compromised magnetosphere. The fact is we have no idea what will happen to our infrastructure, and electronics," Jacob answered.

94

Alice sat back down, glad she now had some understanding, and reference to the numbers and numerous abbreviations they were throwing back and forth at each other. But it didn't matter, if Jacob, Andy and Kevin were right; they could be back in the Stone Age by this time tomorrow night. But if Michael and Bruce were right, then Andy, Kevin and Jacob would be seen as scaremongers, trying to make worse, something that might pass with nothing more than a few blown relays and frustrated drivers because their satnavs had gone down. There was nothing to do now but wait until tomorrow morning, and watch as the event or storm or whatever they had decided to call it unfolded before them. Only then would they know for sure what lay ahead.

As the thoughts ran through Alice's mind the door opened and agent Burton entered. "Okay we're moving you to the living quarters so you can get some rest and be ready for tomorrow. Please follow me."

Agent Burton stood against the door and waved them past him and into the corridor where Agents Anderson and Frakes were waiting. Jacob, Alice and the others followed the agents along the corridors through to the on-site living quarters, from the window Jacob could see his Camry in a parking bay.

"Okay we're here," Special Agent Frakes announced, handing out the room keys. You have been supplied with food and water to last until breakfast tomorrow. We'll be back here at 0'seven hundred hours, to take you down to the RHESSI control room."

"Wait," Alice protested, "you're locking us in here?"

"For your own protection and wellbeing ma'am," the agent answered, "Oh and Mr Miller." Jacob turned to face him. "We've put your cell phone in your car's glove compartment. We have no idea how it got onto the road, but you'll be pleased to know I've checked it, and it works just fine." Jacob felt the man's sarcasm as he spoke.

Alice wanted to protest her civil liberties, but the others including Jacob had already started to enter their own rooms, and besides, she felt exhausted. She had not even recovered from the flight, let alone taken in and organized the day's events in to a logical sequence so that she could at least analyze and understand them. Sighing she smiled back at the agent with a *Fuck you* smile and entered the room. As she stepped through the door was closed and locked.

"So, this is where I am until they let me go," Alice muttered quietly to herself as she walked farther into the room. She looked at the food they had left, lifting and folding the various packages of what Alice would call, *poisoned cardboard processed shit.* "No thanks." Letting the packets fall back onto the table. She sat on the bed and looked at the clock, 12:16 a.m. Sighing she stripped down to her underwear, climbed into the bed, and fell into a deep and troubled sleep.

Chapter 6
Goddard Space Center, RHESSI Building. 6:58 a.m. Local Time

February 24th, 2022.

Alice woke to the banging at the door. Still somewhat dazed and foggy, she sat forward pushing her hair away from her face.

"Okay, okay," she shouted. "Jesus I'm getting up." She whispered to herself in silent protest as she climbed out of the bed and made her way to the bathroom. As she sat on the toilet, the door to her room opened. It was agent Burton.

"Ms Fisher, are you ready to go?"

"Christ, I'm on the loo. I'll be five minutes, let me get washed and dressed," Alice objected.

"Five minutes then Ms Fisher. I'll be outside."

"Yeah, I'm sure you will be."

In the corridor, the agent waited along with the guests that had stayed overnight. The door to room 306 opened and Alice walked out, looking refreshed but hurried and frustrated. She followed Agent Burton as he turned without saying a word, and started along the maze of corridors on their way to the main dining hall.

"I heard you shout you were on the loo?" Jacob said with a childish giggle.

Alice smiled and playfully hit him on his back, "Shut up," she chuckled, "I panicked. One minute I'm having, well you know, a wee, and the next he's in the room like some damn terminator."

"As long as you're finished on, *the loo.*" Jacob laughed again.

Alice didn't respond verbally, she just smirked.

"Breakfast is being served until nine forty-five. I'll be back then to collect you and escort you to the RHESSI control room." Agent Burton allowed them to make to their way into the hall.

"You not eating?" Jacob asked him.

"Already have," the agent replied.

"Yeah, probably the town's children," Alice whispered from behind her hand as they entered the semi-circle of serving cabinets and refrigerators.

They each took a tray. Alice sighed as she picked hers up and slid it along the polished metal bars as she placed breakfast items on it: a glass of orange juice, a bagel, pancakes and two eggs sunny side up. Of course, if she were at home Alice would be having a full English breakfast, including her favorite, black pudding, made with pig's blood. They sat at a reserved table. Jacob, Alice, Kevin and Andy at one side with Bruce and Michael at the other. Alice thought Bruce and Michael looked excluded from her little group even though the FBI were keeping just as close tabs on them, but she elected not to say anything and continued eating her breakfast in silence. Once the plates were cleared the conversation started up.

"Not long now until we know the full extent." Jacob was the first to speak. Alice couldn't help but notice how his hands were clutched tightly together and how his right leg bounced up and down. She'd never seen him this nervous, not even the first night they'd slept together.

Kevin checked his watch. "Its nine thirty-eight. In an hour, we'll know who was right and who was wrong."

"It's not about who's wrong or right. It's about ensuring the proper course of actions and counter measures are taken, and that we actively seek to negate any unnecessary issues that may arise," Michael said.

Andy looked over and laughed in a cynical manner. "Don't give us your bull shit! You were ready to fucking hang us out to dry yesterday. What's the matter now that it's time? Are you worried that you under played what you could see on the model?"

Bruce defended Michael. To Alice it seemed as though the table was divided. "Andy, don't you talk to Michael in that way. Remember who he is, your superior. What we saw in the model doesn't reflect what you interpreted at all; I think you owe him an apology."

But Andy remained defiant. "My superior? I hardly think so, and it'll be you two who apologize to me when we see the model played out."

As tempers flared, and accusations began to be made, the five men started arguing between them. Jacob, Andy and Kevin argued that Bruce and Michael had used this to play a political game. To pander to the White House by agreeing on its view of the lack of potential disasters this coming solar storm would bring. In return, Bruce and Michael accused Jacob, Andy and Kevin of over-reacting, making sensationalist claims and acting unprofessionally.

To Alice it was all childish. Soon, one of their opinions would be proved correct and until the event had passed she saw this argument as nothing more than posturing and jostling for position. And on top of that she was tired, and she'd had enough.

"Shut up! All of you just shut up. You're supposed to be highly educated men. Start acting like it. We don't know what's going to happen and shouting about it and arguing over who's got the biggest dick won't make a dam difference when this thing hits us. I don't know the details. Hell! I barely understood some of what you were talking about last night. All I know is that something is on its way. It could be very bad or it might be just a pain in the backside. But I do know something, if it is bad there are astronauts on the Space Station who may die because of it. I suggest you all grow up and collect yourselves so you can work together. Should the need arise."

The group sat in silence and looked at Alice in the same way her children did. The silence was broken by a single slow applause; they each looked at Agent Burton as he approached the table smiling. He held out his arm pointing it towards the exit.

"Shall we?" he asked.

The group started to make their way to the control room. As Alice passed the agent he complimented her on her people skills.

"Well done, shutting the children up," Agent Burton said.

Alice allowed him one courteous smile and then followed behind the other men, and along the corridors. They entered the RHESSI control room. The room dark compared to the bright spring day outside. The constant buzzing and whirring of the many computers and servers that lined the room was the only noise to break the uneasy silence. Alice looked at her watch and then around the room. Everybody wore the same look of dread as they waited for information from NASA's magnetometer stations and the European Space Agency's four satellites, which monitored the magnetosphere.

10:25 a.m. Local Time.

The first signs of the shockwave interacting with earth's magnetic shields started to show. As the aurora began over the southern hemisphere, the readings from the magnetometer stations started to come through. On one of the larger monitors Commander Relford began to give a running commentary on the view from his unique position, 255 miles above the earth.

"Welcome Commander Relford." Bruce started the conversation as if to prove to Jacob that all was fine, and that his judgment call had been the correct one.

"Hello down there," Commander Relford replied.

"How are things looking up there? Any sign of a shift in the predictions you made?" Bruce asked.

"It's quite amazing. I have never seen an aurora spread this far around the globe. It's as if God himself is putting on his own Fourth of July show."

Bruce turned to one of the technicians monitoring the magnetometer stations. "Can you give me a current reading?" he asked.

The technician checked and answered, "They're reading -180nT at the moment."

Bruce arched his eyebrow at Jacob and then turned back to the screen. "Commander Relford, can you see or are your instruments reading anything we should be worried about down here on Earth?"

"Nothing at all Bruce. I would just enjoy the display. It's not often the big guy puts a show on like this," Commander Relford answered. As he spoke the screen fizzed and shifted with distortion.

Jacob made his way to the desk displaying the storms output. The magnetometer station readings lagged behind what was actually taking place; though they could almost measure and report in real time there was still a small delay. Alice watched as Jacob looked at the screen and then back at Andy and Kevin who had noticed him moving. Jacob's expression didn't fill Alice with the confidence that the commander and Bruce were showing. Jacob moved back and sat next to Alice. The video link to the ISS distorted and then came back.

"It's spiking," he whispered.

"What do you mean?" she asked.

"There's a delay between what's happening, the instruments reading it and then getting the information to us. We haven't seen it yet, but the distortion on the video feed is a sign of what's coming. When I lived in LA, an earthquake struck while I was talking to a friend who lived fifty miles away. It was ten seconds after me when she felt it. That's what's happening here," Jacob replied.

The distortion came back across the screen.

"Commander Relford, we're getting a little distortion down here. How is it up there?" Bruce tried to keep the light-heartedness going.

"It is perfectly normal for communications to suffer during a storm like this."

The image turned blue, displaying no other information than a small banner which read. *No signal. Check Input.* The words bounced slowly around the screen.

"A little disruption is to be expected. The communications will come back on line soon," Bruce said, looking at Michael.

"Bruce, I think you should see this." Jacob waved him over.

"What is it?" Bruce snapped back.

Jacob answered. "The sensors are now reading this storm at -500nT. It's still in the early stage and climbing. This is getting bigger."

"That can't be right. Are you sure?" Bruce asked, agitated. "Michael, check those readings."

"He's right; it's now at -575nT and it's still rising," Michael confirmed.

"Is this why the signal from the ISS cut out?" Alice asked.

"Most probably, but there's no way of knowing until this passes," Andy answered.

"-625nT and rising." Jacob called out the current reading.

Kevin monitored the global positioning system. "GPS is failing," he shouted.

"Where?" Andy shouted back at him.

"It's hard to tell. At least four of the thirty-two satellites are down. No, make that nine, twelve, eighteen. Shit! We've lost twenty-seven satellites."

"Where?" Alice repeated the question.

"Everywhere. They're all down. GPS is gone!"

Jacob up-dated Bruce again with the latest reading from the sensors. "-685nT and still rising."

Bruce marched over to where he sat. "That can't be right!"

Andy now shouted out again, "We're losing communication satellites; the cell network is down."

The control room was now a perfect portrayal of dread. Everything that Jacob had said when Alice had first arrived was coming true, and it was terrifying. Was she watching the collapse of the modern world unfold before her? All of humankind's latest technology appeared to have been torn apart within minutes. Bruce now looked dumb founded; he was clearly at a loss. The man who had sent the first manned mission to Mars now looked like a lost child. Alice understood that he was starting to realize just how bad this was going to be. He'd denied it, fooling himself into discounting Jacob's model as overplaying it; *scaremongering* was the term he'd used. He'd told the White House that the storm would pass with minimal disruption, but now he realized that wasn't the reality of it and he knew he would now have to stand before his peers and admit he was wrong. Alice recognized that to Bruce, that was just as bad as what was happening.

"All civilian based satellite communications are down," Andy shouted out.

"They can't be. There are over eleven-hundred satellites up there" Kevin responded.

"I know, but they're down, they're all gone."

"-725nT," Michael shouted out and then there was nothing but silence. The control room was plunged into darkness and the only sound that could be heard was the whirring down of the many cooling fans used to keep the hardware from overheating. Alice breathed in sharply and reached out to grab Jacob's arm, she needed to know she wasn't alone.

There wasn't much that frightened her, but being alone in the pitch dark while this was happening did. She found his arm and clenched it tight. Alice couldn't stop her mind drifting back to her old home and her two boys. She knew they were five hours behind them and thankfully Rob wouldn't have started the journey to school yet. She found comfort knowing that while this happened to everyone, everywhere, they were at least at home with their father.

"What happens next?" she asked.

"The EMP," Jacob answered, "It's blown the power out. Remember the Hydro-Québec power grid? Well it's happened here. Don't worry; the emergency lighting will kick in soon."

As he spoke the emergency lights flickered to life and the sharp white glow lit the now silent control room. The banks of monitors and computers now lay dormant. All the technology in the room was now useless.

"Is it over?" Alice asked.

"Not yet!" Jacob asked.

"The lights have come on," she said.

"The back generators here are hardened against an EMP, most military facilities are, and NASA uses the same technology."

In the dim light, they looked between each other. All of them wondering what was happening around the world.

Andy spoke first. "Carrington event?" he asked Kevin.

"It's possible." Kevin replied.

"What's the Carrington event?" Alice asked.

"In 1859, the earth was hit by a large storm resulting from a CME like this one. It blew out the small numbers of electrical equipment, and telegraph systems that were operating back then. Some operators were electrocuted and killed by the storms electric-current that travelled through the telegraph wires to their hand sets. It's the biggest storm we know about," Kevin answered.

"Until this one," Andy whispered.

Jacob, Alice, Kevin and Andy looked over to where Michael and Bruce stood. Both of them looked confused and unsure of what they'd just witnessed. They had both been positive that the effects of the storm wouldn't be this bad. They felt confident that what they'd told the President's scientific adviser had been correct, but they'd both been wrong. Now standing in this harshly lit, silent and stale room, the realization of their mistake had hit them both. They looked at each other before turning to the others who looked at them with disappointment and pity. But no one spoke. Jacob saw no reason why he should now criticize them. He, like the others, could see it on their faces. Nothing that Jacob could think of to say would make them feel any worse or make anything better.

Time seemed to stand still for Alice. It had only been seconds, maybe a minute or two at the most since the power had gone out, but it seemed much longer. Her mind scrambled for things to say, anything that would break the uneasy silence, but as she started to form a sentence, Andy spoke up. "We should go outside. See what's happening."

No one else answered or spoke; they just acknowledged Andy and followed him out of the control room and down the short corridor to the exit. Outside the atmosphere seemed strange and Alice instantly recognized the sensation from the last total eclipse she'd witnessed in England, in 1999. It was the same eeriness as that. There was no wind or even a soft breeze. No birds were singing, and everywhere was silent, the air itself seemed charged somehow, as if her body was picking up on the electromagnetism of the storm. Above them the aurora was in full view, brilliant flashes of green and blue raced across the sky in beautiful and mesmerizing patterns. She noticed Jacobs's un-kept hair standing up at the edges and it reminded her of children rubbing balloons on nylon clothes, and then sticking them to their heads.

Kevin pointed to it. "Static."

"You can feel it? The air is charged," Andy said.

It all seemed so surreal, and yet at the same time fascinating and dreamlike. She couldn't imagine how something in nature this wonderful would be so harmful. Alice continued to gaze around the sky. Everywhere she looked was now filled with colored flashes as the particles carried from the sun in the shockwave hit the earth's magnetic field. Agents Burton and Anderson joined them outside, standing next to the group they had been charged to keep at the facility until this event was over.

"Beautiful, isn't it?" Jacob asked them as the stood in silence.

"I've never seen the Northern Lights," Agent Anderson replied.

"You're not seeing them here either," Jacob said.

Agent Anderson pulled Jacob's car keys from his pocket and handed them to him. Their job was done, as far as the FBI was concerned, there was no longer a need to keep them from telling people what was coming, because it was happening in front of them, and it was happening all around the world.

Agent Burton delivered the good news. "Okay, you're all welcome to leave and do whatever you people normally do."

"Does that mean you have finished with us agent?" Alice asked hoping the agent wouldn't pick up on her British sarcasm.

But he did, nodding as if he were tipping an imaginary cowboy hat. "Good day Ma'am," he replied.

They stood for a few minutes longer until the aurora dispersed and the sky once again became a clear blue. The two agents headed back inside the building. With them now seemingly of no further interest to the FBI, Alice turned to Jacob.

"Thank God you have your keys back, I need my bags from your trunk," Alice said

"I'll go get them for you."

Jacob headed toward his Camry, pushing the button on the key fob to open the trunk, but nothing happened. Jacob pressed it again this time harder and pointing it directly at the car but still nothing.

He moved closer and repeated his actions, but the trunk stayed shut and Jacob started to feel an unease swelling up inside him. Moving to the driver's door he placed the key in the lock and turned it, holding his breath. The lock opened, but only on that door; the central locking was not operating. He pulled the door open and sat in the driver's seat. Putting the key into the ignition he turned it and nothing happened. The usual assortment of lights that normally illuminated the dash stayed blank and the V6 engine that normally started on the first flick of the key didn't respond. Jacob feared the worst. Realizing what was happening Andy and Kevin made their way over to Jacob and his stricken car.

"What's up?" Kevin asked he approached the open door.

"It's dead, completely dead," Jacob said as he pulled the hood release.

Andy moved around to the front and lifted the hood. Everything looked as it should, there seemed to be no damage, no signs of burning or charred cables. Andy pulled open the black plastic cover of the battery, he un-clipped the positive terminal and clipped it back into place.

"Try that."

Jacob moved back to the driver's side and flicked the key. This time the engine fired and purred into life. Leaving it running Jacob returned to Andy, who was fastening the battery cover back into its dedicated place.

"Thanks."

"No worries," Andy replied and continued as he dropped the hood down. "Why do you think that happened? The EMP shouldn't have been able to do that."

Alice moved herself next to them. "But didn't you say that's what would happen?"

"I said it might happen, not necessarily that it would happen," Jacob replied.

"But surely if the main power went out." Alice began to ask a question.

"That's not how it works," Andy interrupted, "You have to remember that the mains are constantly on, constantly charged and working at a much higher voltage.

A car is typically only twelve volts, and at the time the EMP hit the car wasn't on, just the clock, alarm and radio settings, that shouldn't be enough to cause a system failure."

As Andy continued his explanation a loud explosion ripped through the peaceful air. Each of them ducked instinctively not knowing where the sound had come from. From behind the main building they could now see a large plume of thick black smoke and Kevin recognized it immediately as burning aviation fuel.

"Shit! What was that?" Alice asked, her voice trembling.

"An aircraft has come down," Kevin answered.

"How close do you think that was?" Jacob asked.

"At least quarter-of-a-mile," Andy said.

"It sounded closer," Alice reasoned.

"If it was, we would have been hit with debris," Kevin reassured her.

In the distance, another explosion boomed and then another, and Jacob realized with horror what was happening.

He turned to Alice and gently took hold of her arm. What he said next sent a shock wave of panic and fear through her. "We have a problem!"

Chapter 7

February 24th, 2022. 10:25 a.m. EST

With the aurora beginning to disperse its heavenly show, the shock wave began to hit the higher orbiting satellites, their circuitry overloaded, rendering them dead. As the shockwave reached the Hubble Telescope, the intensity knocked the telescope from its normal trajectory and on a path that would place it in the grasp of the earth's gravity, causing it to tumble uncontrollably back down.

All orbiting satellites with the exception of the most heavily shielded; U.S. Chinese and Russian military satellites, were now rendered useless, nothing more than worthless hulks of metal orbiting the earth, smashing into each other causing a calamitous chain of events that would see some starting a journey back down to earth, where they would smash on the ground or splash down into any of the earth's oceans. Some were knocked clear of our gravity and would forever be destined to tumble through space.

Some of mankind's greatest technological achievements, the ones we all took for granted every time we made a call, sent an SMS, switched on the TV or radio, or followed the instructions of a satnav, had gone in the blink of an eye. As the EMP continued on its destructive journey, power stations and electrical systems around the world collapsed. With their GPS disabled, the electronic systems that drive the worlds shipping failed, causing all sea going craft: from pleasure yachts to the mightiest of the ocean liners and super tankers, to become nothing more than great steel leviathan's drifting aimlessly in the world oceans. With no hope of immediate rescue, the crews were at the mercy of worlds currents. In the sky, aircraft that had been caught when the EMP had struck had suffered catastrophic engine and system failures causing them to fall back to the ground. Airliners cruising at altitudes of 40,000 feet had lost all power. Even the two redundant systems had failed leaving the pilots with no control. There would be no controlled gliding, and from this altitude the crew and passengers had fifty seconds before the falling aircraft would hit the ground. Fifty seconds to kiss their children, fifty seconds to pray, fifty seconds to tell their family, friends and lovers, *I love you*. And fifty seconds to prepare for death.

On one such flight Steve David found himself clinging to the chair he was strapped in to. Hunted by the media for his supposed leaking of the problems caused by the SOL 1 engines, he'd fled his home. Deciding to hide in Canada until this media frenzy had blown over, or he was able to get Jacob to admit that it was he that had told the English press. But now those thoughts were gone and only one filled his mind; his imminent death. As a former aero engineer before his days with NASA, he knew too well what the chain of events would be when the Boeing 777-300 hit the ground at its terminal velocity. His eyes would barely have time to see and register the impact as the plane crumpled from the nose back to where he sat. As he looked through the small window, the horizon began filling it. Gone was the deep blue sky of high altitude. It was the sky line of Toronto which now filled his vision. The impact came as he'd expected it to. But nothing else registered after the initial jolt.

Cars, trucks and buses had all succumbed to the EMP: from the deserted desert and country roads to the mightiest highways. All traffic everywhere stopped, the ECU's in modern vehicles tripping out. The contact breakers in older vehicles heated to the point of melting. Vehicles on the quieter roads gently glided to a halt. Some were not so lucky. As multiple pile-ups of out-of-control cars and trucks plowed head long into each other, the people trapped in the wreckage would have no help until the emergency services became mobile once again. Trains that ran solely on electricity glided to a halt, stranding passengers en-route. The world's remaining steam engines continued run, but without the signaling systems, they too had to come to a stop. Some passengers were not so lucky, as with the air and road traffic, the breakdown of control systems came at the wrong time for them. Trains due to pass on separate lines hit head on as the electronic points that controlled which tracks they ran on failed to switch. Others couldn't stop in time and hit the bunkers in stations causing the trains to de-rail and wipe the platforms clear of the waiting passengers. Others careered off the tracks on bends and curves they were unable to break for. In Japan, the MLX-01 Maglev train could no longer be suspended and propelled by the immensely powerful magnets. At 355 mph it fell back onto the rails, causing the carriages to tumble and concertina.

Office blocks, department stores, schools and hospitals fell into a dark silence. Elevators full of people stopped mid journey, some hidden inside the building walls and interiors, and some in external glass elevators were now stuck between floors, and with no way out they hung off the side of buildings, stranded and powerless as they watched the chaotic events unfold beneath them on the ground and in the skies above. Miners were caught underground, their only way back to the surface was the vertical mine shafts, some reaching over two miles.

The filtration and water pump systems also failed allowing water to take back the shafts, while the air became thick, old, stale and unbreathable. Operating theatres around the world were plunged into darkness, and the robotic systems now used during the most delicate of procedures stopped working. There was no emergency backup. In the ICU and critical care wards, ventilators and life support systems died, taking their dependent patients with them.

The powerful computers that controlled the world's economies also stopped, cash machines, debit and credit card devices ceased to operate. No one had access to money, and the few that still carried sufficient cash realized quickly it would be best to keep it hidden.

Animals fared no better. Migrating birds found themselves miles off course, some too far out at sea to be able to make it back to land. Whales also lost their way while they travelled to their mating and calving grounds. The biggest of the oceans predators found themselves lost and confused. Great White Sharks that travel from Baja California to Hawaii, to the White Shark Café, become lost and disorientated. Land animals also found themselves confused and out-of-place. The extra sensory instincts and abilities that animals have sensed the change. Domestic prey animals hid, while the predators we share our homes with became frightened and aggressive. Dogs and cats attacked their owners and each other as the same EMP that had overloaded our sensitive electrical systems played havoc with theirs.

The instruments and warning mechanisms aboard the ISS had sounded as the shock wave had sped toward it on a collision course. Commander Relford ordered his crew to the chamber built in to the space station for events such as this, but he knew that no one during the design stage had ever envisioned such a huge eruption would come at a time when the magnetic shields that protected the earth, and the station, would be in such a weakened state. As he locked the heavily protective door and looked at his fellow astronauts, all of whom had become his friends, he also knew it wouldn't protect them from the levels of radiation the coming storm would bring.

The station shuddered and groaned in protest when the solar winds hit it. Instruments and operation panels blew out in a frenzy of sparks and thick foul-smelling smoke. The only systems built with the shielding that was able to stand up to such an onslaught were the life support systems, and even these systems had largely switched over to the backups. Pushed out toward deep space from its low earth orbit with the ease a child would push a toy car, the space station was now adrift and out of the reach and protection of earth's gravity. With only emergency power, Commander Relford sent a single encrypted communication to the crew of SOL1 who were completely unaware of the events that were taking place on earth. The message read:

FOR COMMANDER SOL 1
From
Commander Relford International Space Station
Earth hit by massive shock wave resulting from CME. Most if not all satellites inoperable. ISS damaged beyond repair & out of earth orbit. Unable to contact NASA. Cannot penetrate the shockwave. Suggest you do not attempt to return to earth. Not sure what state they're in. Strongly suggest that you wait to receive orders from NASA before taking any action. Remain in the main habitat.

The shockwave will hit Mars in approximately 34 hours.

God, bless you all.
ISS out.

The storm lasted for several hours and the auroras could be seen in almost every country, and on every continent. As the last of them faded, the billions of people worldwide who had been drawn outside to watch nature's great show of strength and power made their way back into their darkened and quiet homes and places of work.

With the storm now over and the energy from it dispersed, power stations started to reboot and the world began to emerge from its temporary Stone Age. But the devastation that had been caused had cost untold lives and trillions of dollars of damage to our infrastructure and economy.

February 24th, 2022. 5:43 p.m. EST.

Back inside the starkly lit control room, Bruce and Michael headed toward the main server system, on which all the other desktop PC's and systems relied. Hesitantly, and with a heavy a sigh, Bruce pulled the main trip switch down into the charge position on the control panel. Looking back at Michael, he grasped the trip switch that had jumped into the off position.

With a loud metallic clank, he pushed it back into the on position and instantly the control room burst back into life. The fans started to whirr back up to speed, and the harsh lighting was replaced by the much softer ceiling spot lamps. Each screen came to life, each of them showed their own boot up sequence followed by the now familiar log in screens. Kevin, Andy and Jacob helped Michael and Bruce to log in to each terminal.

"You still stand by what you told the President's adviser?" Jacob asked Bruce.

Bruce wore a look of embarrassment and frustration as he turned to Jacob. He could see that Kevin and Andy had joined Jacob where he stood. "You think this is the time to be a fucking smart ass?"

Jacob shook his head softly as he answered. "No, it's not a question of who was right or wrong in this room. It is question of how many lives have been lost because the wrong information was given to the President. If he'd been told what he should have been told."

Bruce cut Jacob off mid-sentence. "What if he'd been told what? No one knew this would happen. There was no precedent for a storm this big; we had no way of knowing our systems and satellites would be so vulnerable to it."

"Bullshit!" Jacob replied angrily. "You had the same data we did, we fucking told you, but you weren't interested in the truth, it was obvious from the data RHESSI obtained before it went down. No! For you and Michael it was all about agreeing with the President's adviser, scoring brownie points to further your career, and now people have died who didn't need to."

"How do you reckon that?" Michael asked.

This time it was Andy that answered, "Because if you had told the adviser what you both knew to be right, they would have had time to ground all aircraft, put running road blocks on the highways and stop the trains, even if only some lives had been saved."

"Do you know how long all of that would have taken; there would have been no way of stopping everything. It would have cost millions of dollars and would have been futile. And if we'd been wrong, then what?" Bruce answered.

"What?" Jacob asked. "You heard the sounds outside, the sounds of cars crashing, and the screeching of aircraft as they fell from the sky. We don't need to wait until these systems are back on line. We know that this happened locally so there's no logical reason it shouldn't have also happened worldwide."

"Assuming their advisers hadn't ignored the truth," Kevin mumbled under his breath.

As the last words left Kevin's mouth the systems finished rebooting and were now online and available. Alice watched as they all stopped their blame game and started pouring through the screens of data. Alice approached Kevin.

"Are the phones working? I need to call Rob. I need to check on my family" she asked.

Kevin pointed to a wall mounted phone. She lifted the hand set and with a nervous and shaking hand dialed her home. After a few notes of connection, she heard the repetitive ring tone as the call waited patiently to be answered.

"Hello." Rob's voice came softly through the handset pressed to her ear.

"Rob, Rob its Alice." She tried to control the emotional wobble in her voice as she started to talk to him.

"Oh God, Alice. I feared you had gone down in a transatlantic flight. It's so good to hear your voice."

"How are the boys?" Alice asked.

"They're good, it hit before the school run thankfully. I'm just glad you weren't in the air."

"They offered me a lift to the airport, but the car wouldn't start so I had to stay. Then, soon after, we started to hear the crashes on the freeway and aircraft falling out of the sky. It was awful, all those poor souls."

"Why were there still planes flying, isn't it the job of NASA and the European Space Agency to warn the governments of things like this?"

Alice covered the mouth piece and leaned into the wall mounted phone booth. "They did know. I got a call from my contact, that's why I'm here, they knew this storm was coming and it was dismissed by the President's own adviser and the boss at RHESSI and Martialis," she whispered.

"Shit. What are you going to do?"

"For now, nothing, we've already had the FBI lock us in here until the storm passed in case we started a panic," Alice answered, cautiously.

"I'm not sure I like this Alice, it's one thing to report what you're told but to be in the middle of it. Especially with things you hear about the FBI."

"This needs to be reported Rob, that's what I am, you know that."

"And if you disappear, then what? What do I tell the boys?" Rob asked.

"You've been reading too much *James Patterson*. I don't think things like that happen. Besides I'm keeping quiet until I'm back in the UK."

"Does this mean you're coming back soon?"

"I don't know when flights will resume after this chaos. I'll be here a while I think, at least this way I can gather what I need," Alice answered.

"And what about your contact? Won't that get you into trouble?" Rob asked.

"There are bigger things to worry about."

The phone became quiet for a few seconds before Alice spoke again. "Is the TV back on at home yet?"

"No, just the landlines, I guess they're working through the old Atlantic cables. Everything else is off, the internet, mobile phones, everything. Even the dam car won't start."

"So long as you're all ok. I have to go. I'll check back later. Give my love to the boys."

"Take care," Rob said as Alice hung up.

She turned away from the phone and looked back at the five men that she had been with during what was undoubtedly the worst human crisis that mankind had faced as a species. There had been events that had seen countries, even continents thrown into chaos, but never the whole planet and our entire civilization at the same time. How had she come to end up in this dark room with these five people who now argued with each other, blaming each other while the world outside was in utter disarray? She was exhausted from it all; hearing that her boys were ok had swept away the worry of her own personal tragedy. But what surprised her was the relief she felt when she heard Rob's voice. Perhaps it was just the emotion of the last few hours and tomorrow she would feel the same as she did when she'd decided to leave him. But for now, she wasn't sure. Somewhat fortunate for Alice there was a large black leather sofa in the room. As she lay on it and made herself comfortable she watched Jacob, Andy, Bruce, Kevin and Michael as they began looking at charts and graphs. For now, at least, it seemed the data that had started coming in had distracted them for their argument. Alice felt herself becoming relaxed and drained of the last reserves of energy she had and with the office noise becoming nothing more than a background din and the sounds of conversation becoming ever more distant, Alice fell asleep.

On board, the ISS Commander Relford and the three crew members fought to keep the station in one piece. The ISS had maneuvering capabilities. It had to have, to ensure that it could move away from any space debris that orbited the earth. Pieces as small as a half penny, traveling at speeds in excess of 8km/s would puncture the skin of the station causing decompression resulting in complete structural failure. In its low earth orbit the responsibility of predicting when and where this debris may hit the station was the responsibility of The U.S. Space Surveillance Network. But moving the station took time, sometimes days to complete, it wasn't designed to be agile. All of the stations photovoltaic arrays along the left truss structure had separated under the immense strain of the shockwave. The arrays on the right side were only twenty percent operable, and that wasn't enough to support the systems needed for human survival.

The European experimental module along with the mating adapter had also been lost. Other areas too, including the Japanese experimental module and centrifuge module had sustained breaches which had opened them up to outer space. The crew was now confined to the U.S. habitation module which had no access to the one escape pod. Heating, drinking water and oxygen were now finite. What they had was all they were going to have, the stations ability to produce clean water and breathable air had gone when the initial shockwave had hit. For the four crew members, the fact they'd survived the impact at all was a miracle. But as they now drifted away from the earth in the smashed and stricken station they each began to realize that it may have been better to have died quickly. Dehydration wouldn't be what would kill them. The human body can last three days without water, but only three hours without shelter enough to keep hyperthermia at bay and only three minutes without air. Either death would not be quick or painless. As the last of the systems and lights started to fail the four of them sat in silence. What could any of them say as they faced certain death together in the void of space? What words would make it less painful and more bearable? Only the crying of the station's lead scientific researcher was heard. Commander Relford reached a decision and leant forward, placing his right hand on the latch that held the main door to the European experiment module.

They all knew that it was gone, and on the other side of the door was only the vacuum of space. The other three gently placed their hands on Commander Reliford's arm. He looked between them, and all of them had the same resigned look on their faces. They recognized they faced a choice between asphyxia, hyperthermia or an almost instant and painless death outside. "It's been honor," Relford said as he turned the latch. Before any of the crew had time to respond to his last words, they were pulled from the station.

Alice woke from her impromptu slumber. Jacob was sat at the end of the sofa holding a coffee. She looked around the room and saw Kevin and Andy standing by one of the servers while Michael and Bruce were deep in conversation at the far end of the room. She yawned and stretched.

"How long was I out?" she asked Jacob.

"Two, maybe three hours."

"Any news on how bad it was?" she asked, regaining her consciousness.

"It's bad. Trading has ceased on all of the world markets and the banking system has all but collapsed."

"I meant what's the human cost?" she asked.

"Worse, we don't know and I guess we won't for some time to come. Remember it took FEMA three days to get water to a stadium after Hurricane Catrina, and that was with a full working infrastructure. That's all but gone now."

"All-but?" Alice asked.

"What?"

"You said all but, what's still operational?" she asked.

"The military's hardware is hardened against EMPs in case of a nuclear strike, for the moment they're the only ones with full communications and transport. So, they're in charge," he said.

"Fucking great, that's what we need in a time of humanitarian crisis. The Generals in charge," she replied.

"It'll be the same everywhere, even in the UK."

"Guess it will be!"

He was right, the civilian government and police forces were unable to cope with an event like this. Their equipment had not been designed to withstand such a massive EMP spike because it had always been assumed that anything that big would have been the result of a nuclear war. And in that scenario, there would be no civilian government or police force. So, for now the military would be in charge. And to Alice that was like putting the kids in charge of the weekly shopping.

"How is everyone?" she asked Jacob.

"We're all shell-shocked. Trying to get a hold of family and friends, but it's a mess out there. Even our not-so-friendly FBI agents have left. Guess we're not so important after all."

"And you?"

"Much the same, sick to my stomach. I've been sick I'm not sure how many times."

"Is there anyone else that can help?"

"We have tried to get hold of Steve David. He was one of the lead engineers on the Martialis project. If we can get him on board it'll be a big help."

124

"Maybe I can help with that. I'd like to talk to him anyway."

"Good idea," Jacob answered.

Jacob stood and walked over to where Kevin and Andy were standing. With a new task and something to focus on other than getting home, which she knew wouldn't be happening anytime soon, Alice stood and headed for the room she'd stayed in the previous night. She needed to have a shower and change. As she walked along the corridor she could see outside the windows, and it was pitch black. Night had rolled in while she'd slept and with the local power stations still down no street lamps or office lamps had come on. The roads too were silent and void of any traffic headlamps or even the soft red glow of tail lamps. In her room, only a few of the lamps operated, the buildings systems only allowed certain items to draw power from the generators. Air conditioning in the accommodation part was not seen as necessary, but at this time of the year, that wasn't so important.

Alice saw little point in doing anything to find Steve David tonight. It seemed obvious that the best plan would be to have a good night sleep and start fresh in the morning. Though with no transport, electricity or internet, she wasn't entirely sure how she would start.

As the day came to an end and Alice slept, the toll on the planet and on mankind could not yet be measured. Many people had lost family and friends. It wasn't just humanity that suffered; it was what we were that had also so very nearly been lost.

February 25th. 8:45 a.m. EST. Goddard Space Center.

Jacob woke on the couch Alice had slept on the previous day. Once the generators had kicked in and data had started to come in from around the country and from what few satellites were still in operation things had become hectic. But he had woken to a different world from the one he'd woken to only 24 hours earlier. He sat upright and rubbed his eyes yawning as he did. On the other chairs, Andy and Kevin were starting to wake. They both looked as exhausted as he felt.

"Morning," he said, still half yawning.

"Morning." Andy muttered in reply.

Kevin didn't answer verbally; he waved his hand to them both and nodded as he pushed his hair from his eyes.

"Is there anything to eat?" Andy asked.

"There'll be food in the hall," Jacob answered.

"Sounds like a plan," Kevin said.

The three men walked to the hall and grabbed what packets of cereal and fruit they could. Though it had only been yesterday and the fresh food and milk hadn't yet spoilt, they knew it would only be a few days before they would be down to tins and packets. As they sat eating Bruce and Michael entered and sat with them.

"I wonder what today will bring?" Bruce said, staring his breakfast.

"For us, more of the same, sifting through scattered accounts and incomplete data. For those outside and across the country, God only knows." Andy answered.

As they ate Alice joined them. "Hi," she said as she sat with them. The five men replied in kind.

"Any developments?" she asked.

"That depends." Bruce answered.

"Depends?"

"Whether what we tell you finds its way into your newspaper," Bruce replied.

"You're kidding, right?"

"No," Bruce said flatly.

"The world has gone to shit, I can't get home to see my family and I can't even email or communicate with my paper, and you're worried about me running a story?"

"That's not a bad idea," Andy said.

"What?" Michael asked.

"If Alice stayed with us and reported our efforts, post event, it would at least document it for posterity."

Bruce sighed. This was a good idea and he knew it should be recorded. Future generations would look back on this and having a scientific reporter that had an understanding of not only the event, but how it came about would be the correct thing to do from an historical point of view. "Okay, but I see what you're writing and I have overall editorial control over what you print."

"Agreed. But for now, Jacob has asked me to locate Steve David. I think that should be the priority. What do you think Bruce?" Alice asked him, knowing she was being a little sarcastic. And it wasn't lost on the others.

"Of course, Alice," Bruce replied.

After breakfast, they returned to the control room to analyze the incoming data. As the world started to count the cost it became obvious that those countries that had yet to be a part of the technological world, the developed countries took for granted, had been least affected by the event. The effects would come to those areas a short time later, but they would come and, it would be just as costly. Food and medicine deliveries to the refugee camps in

Syria had stopped as the civilian transports the coalition forces needed no longer worked.

The EMP hardened military vehicles were insufficient in numbers. Famine hit areas in Africa were also starting to see the effects, as Oxfam, and other charities were no longer able to get fresh water and aid to the outlying villages that so badly needed it. In the northern hemispheres winter still had its cold grasp around the globe, and with heating system failures, people in developed countries faced the real possibility of freezing to death in their own homes. The industrial freezers that stored vast quantities of foods for supermarkets had failed, and the back–up generators that hadn't been hardened against an EMP failed to take over allowing the food to spoil. As with everywhere, deliveries to the supermarkets and shops had ceased, and the shelves were soon emptied by those that believed this was to be the end. The delivery trucks that had broken down en-route were ransacked, as were medical supplies. Home ventilators had failed, and with emergency vehicles inoperable, countless more people that relied on them died. Some died alone, and in the dark.

Drinking water supplies had stopped as had sewage treatment, and in the turbulent weather that followed the solar storm, streets around the country over flowed with effluence, providing the perfect breeding ground for disease. With the world back in the Stone Age teams around the country worked tirelessly to try and restart civilization. It was the same across the world, in every country and in every town. The event had left its scars upon the world. Families had lost loved ones, and businesses had failed.

Museums had suffered too, artifacts recovered from the sea bed that had to be stored at precise temperatures and humidity began to decay in the dry air. Works of art, and medieval tapestries stored in air tight and temperature-controlled environments had succumbed as the systems that kept the centuries of deterioration away failed. As the insurance companies added up the financial costs into trillions, the human cost was, as always much higher, and as always, no figure could be put on that.

People of all faiths prayed to their Gods during the event, and people who had shunned the notion of a deity controlling their every move, turned to one, and clung to any hope that it gave them that the world would survive. While some turned to a God, others turned away, questioning again how a loving and forgiving being would take loved ones and friends in such dreadful ways.

Some postulated that nature was readdressing the balance of power, and that the storm which came from out of the blue was indeed a show of force. A warning that mankind must change its ways or suffer the consequences. Others believed malevolent beings from far off galaxies were to blame, and that Scientology had now been proven beyond doubt.

Others looked to the Mayan calendar, sighting that we had interpreted it incorrectly and that 2022 was the year mankind's rule would end. But even as the world debated and argued whether it was more than an unusually large eruption from the Sun, life slowly started to become normal once again, and as with all disasters the human race has faced, be it natural or by our own hands, mankind as a whole had survived and so started the return to our ordinary existence. Scientists now sought to comfort people by saying the odds of any further catastrophes on this scale were incalculable.

In the wake of what had happened, countries around the world put together teams of their best scientists. The President of the United States assembled his own team whose members' only duty was to study the event in minute detail. The President's own scientific adviser personally requested Michael and Bruce to part of the investigation, and while the President had at first been skeptical about his choice he did agree to it. He made them the head of the team, and they in turn appointed Kevin and Andy. Bruce reinstated Jacob, who'd accepted the post on the condition that Alice was brought on board to be the official documenter of the task force.

With the loss of the ISS, and NASA unable to mount any kind of a rescue mission during the event, a day of remembrance for the lost souls aboard the International Space Station had been set for February 24th the following year. It was a date on which the nations that had been represented aboard the ISS would forevermore remember their lost souls. NASA had eventually contacted the Martialis crew and informed them of what had taken place.

They had discussed in length the value of continuing their mission and had decided, after much thought, and assurances that their families had not been casualties of the event, that they would stay until the original planned return date of May 2024.

In Whitehall, London, Prime Minister Daw Kamryn had chaired countless meetings of COBRA, the UK's contingency committee. Included in these meetings were the senior figures of government departments such as

Defense, the Department of Health and the Department for Food and Rural Affairs amongst others. Civil un-rest had largely been less than they had expected, with riots and looting mainly concentrated in the usual hot spots where the anti-government riots had taken place in August 2011. Unlike then, however, this time the home secretary had no choice but to involve the army to help an already depleted police force. Across other areas of the UK the more rural and affluent communities had pulled together, sharing resources and expertise to keep life as normal as possible, showing again the true British spirit that had once been so evident during the Nazi blitzkrieg.

As the weeks rolled into months, and the world recovered, the team of five men and Alice that had been hastily put together continued their work. After weeks of searching and waiting for communications to be fully restored and bodies to be identified, Alice had discovered the fate of Steve David. It had hit Jacob hardest, partly because he was his friend, but mostly because he felt responsible.

If he hadn't had mentioned his concerns to Alice on that morning in the hotel room Steve wouldn't have been fired, and might well be with them now contributing to their efforts. But as with most regrets it was futile to wish for it to be different. And Jacob knew like countless people around the world the pain and guilt would pass in time.

December 31st, 2022. 11:59 p.m. GMT.

As 2022 finally came to an end, the people of the world looked forward to the start of a new year, and a chance to draw a line under the events that had affected every person in every country. For these reasons the celebrations were much more poignant and genuine. It was evident that this New Year's Eve was not an excuse for drunken escapades. And as the world woke to January 1st, 2023, it seemed calmer, more at peace with itself. It was completely the contrary reaction the governments around the world had feared. The riots and unrest had been short lived. Once power had been restored and the infrastructures were able to function once again, the mass revolting and rampaging they had all feared did not happen. Somehow the world had taken the devastating event as a wakeup call in the way that someone who is given the news of a terminal illness does. What was important to their own quality of life was not what they had thought it to be, and with almost global unity the vast majority of people made special and very personal New Year Resolutions.

In what was our darkest hour the human race had risen to the challenge in an unprecedented show of unilateral peace and harmony. Mankind as a race and as a species had shown acts of kindness and empathy for our fellow man that had never been seen before in all of human history.

Perhaps it was this new found human optimism, and the sense that through tragedy we had rediscovered this Eden that we had taken for granted and almost destroyed through our acts of natural vandalism, and the need to feed our ever-growing necessity for material items, that made us realize we are not the masters of all we see. That we are not the indestructible pinnacle of evolution that we had thought our technology had made us. And maybe because we believed that Mother Nature had dealt us her mightiest blow to castigate us for our crimes against her, that for the briefest of moments we stopped looking. Conceivably, it was for all of these reasons, and more that we failed to see the real threat.

Chapter 8

February 5th, 2023.
McGill Artic Research Station (M.A.R.S) North Pole.

John Findley, the base camp manager, was following his usual routine of preparing the camp for the months between March and August when it was open for use.

The research station is found at $79^{\circ}26'$ N, $90^{\circ}46'$ W, on the Axel Heiberg Island, Nunavut. During the months, it was open it provided valuable shelter for around fourteen people from all over the world, while they carried out every possible experiment and expedition. Closed since the end of last season, John along with his Deputy Manager Janet Woods and their Inuit Field assistant Akycha now raced against time to make the camp ready for the first of this year's research teams. John was a veteran manager, having been at the base for the last twelve seasons. During the closed time, he lived in Resolute Canada, just off the ironically named Sunset Strip. He was a tall athletic man. Living this far north there was no place for the obese and unfit. It wasn't just a life style choice to be fit and healthy here, it was a matter of survival. During the winter months when the station was closed John would keep himself clean shaven and his hair short and neat while he was home in Resolute, but when the station opened he would always allow his beard to grow thick and long, with whiskers starting high on his cheek bones and continuing down to the base of his neck. It was the best way to keep frost bite at bay even though these were the summer months. His tangled black and grey beard would often be the butt of the joke for the regulars who travelled to M.A.R.S each year but John was too thick skinned and field hardened to let the odd wise-crack bother him.

And it was often he that had the last laugh when the fresh-faced and clean-shaven researchers suffered sore and agonizing frost bite. Even in the summer months, temperatures seldom climbed above freezing and would often fall as low as 12`F. For his assistant manager, however, growing a beard was not one that Janet could choose.

He'd hired her not just for her academic qualifications but also because of her physical and mental strength. John witnessed some of the hardest men he'd known crack with the isolation and continuous hours of night and day. They sat in the canteen area ready to dig into their first meal of the season.

"How's the food?" John asked as Janet took the first mouthful.

"Oh, it's okay."

"So, what did you do during the closed season?" John asked again.

"Like most people after the event, I attended far too many funerals." Her grin slipped from her face as she answered him. "You? How was your down time?"

John thought before he answered. His mother and father had died when he was a young child in a car wreck, and as an only child he was raised by his uncle and aunt, both of whom died when he was in his early twenties. With no family of his own he was spared the tragedy of the loss of loved ones in the event.

His main concern had been keeping warm while the storm kept the town's electricity supply and back-up generators inactive.

While that had been a major concern for all those that lived in Resolute, he understood that next to Janet, it would sound somewhat selfish and pitiful to compare the inconvenience he'd suffered to her anguish of burying loved ones and friends. During the event, as it had come to be known, Janet's mother and father were travelling back from a vacation to Europe. When the storm hit and the electromagnetic pulse had washed over their airliner, it had lost all power and ditched into the Atlantic. Like everywhere on the planet, the event had happened without any warning, and with the confusion that followed it had taken three days for Janet to be told of her parent's fate. So instead he shook his head, sighed, and thought of a way he could change the subject to keep them both focused on getting the station ready.

"I've fueled all the generators and checked the power supply cables. So far, they're looking good. I need to check the water heaters and radiators to make sure we can keep the place warm."

Janet nodded, knowing he'd changed the subject. She didn't try and bring it back around. She respected John for it, and besides it was still too painful for her to talk about it in any detail.

"Okay, while you do that I'll make sure the Wi-Fi is up and running. The last thing we need is a bunch of scientists and geeks complaining they can't watch their favorite episode of Star Trek." She said with a soft giggle.

"The Harvesting," John replied.

"The what?"

"I believe it's this season's big sci-fi horror hit, The Harvesting, aliens and zombies and such."

"Oh great. We have six months of that to suffer. It's bad enough when they argue whether Star Trek is better than Star Wars, and whether it's Kirk or Picard."

John laughed and responded, "It's easy, Picard. Anyway, it can be worse you know."

"How?" Janet asked still smiling.

"They might discuss Star Wars all season, or even bring a copy of *The Thing*."

Janet hated the thought of that mixture more than the zombie discussions she would have to endure.

"Oh God, I'd not thought of that. For all our sake if that comes with this season's DVD supply send them back, or better still bury them outside somewhere."

They both laughed as they cleared away their lunch plates while continuing their discussion about the glut of terrible movies they'd been receiving in the mail for the station's recreation room. When they'd finished cleaning, John made his way to the operations area of the station where the heating systems were located. Left on a low setting during the stations down time to stop the system freezing in the harsh Arctic winters, it was time to turn up the settings to make the station habitable and safe for human occupation. John checked each individual warm air duct and radiator, ensuring no part of the building would be cold. A single breakdown in only one area would jeopardize the entire station.

Janet made her way to the communication building where she rebooted the station's banks of servers and communications equipment. One by one the LCD screens that had been blank for so long flickered into life, displaying the status of each individual computer until they were all ready to be logged onto the network. Janet entered the stations password *THE RED PLANET 1*, named after the stations acronym M.A.R.S. With the internal systems now operational, they made their way outside to clear the helipad and to get the snow cats as ready as they would ever be. As she continued to check the oil levels in the snow cats, she noticed Akycha approaching the garage smiling and waving, Janet returned the greeting and shouted to him.

"Welcome Akycha, how are you and your family?"

Akycha smiled as he entered the garage. He'd worked at the station during the summer season for enough years now to speak sufficient English to get by. In the early days, he'd tried to teach the station workers the local dialect, Inuktitut, and though Janet and John grasped the basics and could hold a simple conversation, the complexity of the language and frequency of the visitor rotations made it all but impossible, and so he learned English, the language that the vast majority of the scientists who used the station seemed to speak, even if it was their second language.

As Akycha approached he greeted Janet in the customary way of the Kunik by placing his nose and upper lip on Janet's forehead. This greeting was kept only for Janet. As the only female worker here he felt rather protective of her. Though he had his own family he'd known Janet for as long as he'd worked at the station. For everyone else including John, he greeted them with the Chimo, which involved Akycha circling his left hand over their chest, above the heart.

"You need a help?" Akycha asked.

"No thank you, I'm almost finished here."

"Is there much work to be finished?" he asked Janet in his broken accent.

"There is one job left to do before the camp is ready. We need to re-align the satellite dish." She pointed at it and made circular patterns as she did. "The last storm blew it off its orientation."

Though Janet wasn't completely sure he'd understood what she'd said, she reached inside her kit pack and pulled out a bright yellow coated device, and Akycha knew instantly what it was and how to use it. He took it from her hand and turned to face the dish. He walked toward the communication building. Janet watched him walk away pushing the little yellow-plastic coated device into his pocket. As he scaled the ladder she stopped paying attention. She didn't need to worry about him. This was a regular task for him following any powerful whiteouts. Besides, Akycha, like the rest of his people was strong and hardened to the conditions this far north. With her back now turned she dropped the small flimsy yellow hood of the snow cat and put away the tools she'd used. Behind her Akycha climbed the attached ladder. He stepped onto the roof and made his way to the dish where he plugged the re-alignment instrument and unfastened the locking mechanism.

Looking down at the five-inch screen, it showed the dish was off by seven degrees to the North and three degrees to the west. Moving the dish in its cradle until both readings read zero, he snapped the fasteners tight and unplugged the reader. Standing up-right he took time to take in the view around him. He'd lived here all of his life but the beauty and desolation still mesmerized him, he'd spent time in large cities, and he understood the draw they had for people to live there, but he much preferred this idyllic, if sometimes deadly place he proudly called home.

Akycha considered himself to be a fortunate man and a wealthy man by any measure. He was thankful he had a loving wife, children and family around him. As far as he was concerned he lived in paradise and relied on no one, but himself. The event last year had little effect on him and his family. Though they'd lost power, their home still retained its traditional open fire which they used for cooking, heating and for hot water. Whilst they'd lost the convenience of running water for a few weeks life for them carried on much the same. With the plentiful hunting grounds of the ice shelf, he had what he thought many of the visitors to this place were seeking: true contentment.

He turned for the ladder and watched as Janet made her way from the garage toward the main entrance of the accommodation block, and though he knew she couldn't see him, he waved to her as she rounded the corner and disappeared. As he took his first step he felt uneasy on his feet, stopping, he grabbed at the metal framework that supported the various communication apparatus and receivers. It felt as if the skin on his head was tightening, causing pain to circulate around it, he felt dizzy and nauseas, his arms and legs tingled and his breath became short and he fought for air.

His pulse became rapid and whilst he still had cognitive thought, he recognized the symptoms as acute mountain sickness, but how could this be? This only occurred above 8000 feet. Confusion began to take hold as he fought to understand why he felt like this. Akycha, started making his way toward the ladder. If this was AMS he would need to get off the roof and find help before the more severe symptoms started. Stumbling forward, every step was a fight to keep standing and to breathe. Disoriented he reached the edge of the roof, but his reach for the ladder was a lunge, with no measurement of distance or coordination.

Akycha fell off the roof, his body tumbling until he hit the frozen ground with the inevitable thud. He lay still and silent until one large gulp of the now oxygen rich air filled his lungs. His eyes widened and his chest heaved, he lay staring at the bright deep blue sky, as he did he felt his head start too clear as the tingling retreated. His mind scrambled to understand how the air might be so different between the ground and the height of the satellite dish but he had no answers. Pulling himself up he clambered to his feet. Sore and aching from the fall he stepped forward and felt a sharp pain. Wincing, he placed his hand on the spot where the pain radiated. He could feel blood escaping from a wound in his right side. Moving his hand toward his jacket pocket he pulled the yellow reader out and stared at the aerial, which was now only half the length it had been. He knew the aerial had impaled him, and he needed help, he needed the hospital back in Resolute, but first he would have to make it to the main building where he hoped Janet and John would be.

In the main hall, Janet's hand released her grip on the light bulb, and as it came to life she turned to John.

"See it only takes one woman to change a light bulb."

John laughed. "Aye, it only takes one woman, so long as there's one man supervising."

Janet gave an exaggerated sigh. She put away the step ladders and locked the cupboard.

"That's it; the center is now ready for the visitors. Everything that should be warm is, and thanks to Akycha the satellite TV will keep people occupied and all being well, quiet."

As the words left her mouth Akycha burst through the hall doors and fell to his knees holding out his right arm. Janet could tell he was trying to say something, but the air had been taken from his lungs. The harder he gasped and strained to talk, the less audible he was. John recognized that Akycha was suffering from the after effects of AMS. John had spent seasons climbing the highest of peaks and he'd seen people die, and come too close to dying from this hidden killer. As Janet put her arm around him to lift him, she felt the warmth of the blood that continued to escape his body.

"Oh Christ, he's bleeding." She shouted to John.

Their medical training took over from the irrational and alarming thoughts that dominated their minds. Putting him into the recovery position Janet made sure he had a clear air-way while John looked for the wound.

"Got it!" He yelled. "It looks like he impaled himself on something, I'll put pressure on it; you get the first aid kit and a pressure bandage, and call the health center in Resolute. Tell them we need an airlift. Tell them it's Akycha. You tell them down there it's an emergency. We need the chopper!"

Janet understood what he meant. The health center was sometimes reluctant to send the chopper. The

M.A.R.S center had above basic medical facilities, it was necessary because the weather could change in the blink of an eye, and sometimes it wasn't possible to airlift the injured out. They also knew that Janet and John both had medical training, and skills which were almost equal to a paramedic. But this was different; Akycha needed more attention than they had the facilities and training for. Janet tossed the pressure bandaging to John and then ran to the communications room. Tuning into the health center's frequency, she grabbed the mic and pushed the talk button.

"Hello are you there? It's Janet at M.A.R.S. We have a medical emergency, Akycha is injured. John wants immediate evac! Over."

There was just static at first, and then the reply came back.

"Janet? Nick here, how bad is it? Over."

"He needs immediate evac. Over."

"I'll dispatch the chopper now. It'll be with you in around three hours. There's a slight head wind. Over."

"Thanks Andrew, we'll have him ready for transport. Just tell the pilot to push it hard. Over."

"Will do. Over and Out."

Janet sighed with relief as she left the comms room and headed back. She hadn't had to argue with Andrew to get the helicopter, as she'd feared would be the case. She entered the medical bay where she found John seated next to Akycha in one of the three beds. now comfortable and able to breath with the help of a small tube that past air under his nose, Janet smiled at Akycha, and pulled his blankets over him, keeping him warm.

"Are you feeling any better?" she whispered to him.

"Yes, much better now Janet."

"What did they say?" John asked.

"Well it must be my female charm, but he agreed to send to the chopper with none of the usual bullshit." Janet replied.

"How long before it's here?"

"Around three hours. We should leave him to rest." Janet peered over to the now restful Akycha. "I'll see if I can work out what happened to him."

John nodded "Okay, I'll stay here with him." He settled into the chair next to the bed.

Pulling on her cold weather gear, Janet stepped through the door and into the brilliant white landscape. As she walked around the building she followed the now frozen blood trail left by Akycha, and she could see the manic foot prints left by someone who was struggling to walk. She witnessed this kind of straggling, clumsy almost infant like walking many a time while in Resolute, but not by the injured. It was without exception the drunken workers as they tried to pass their final night of being in such a desolate place before returning home for two weeks only for the cycle to start over.

She continued until she stood facing the communications building. From here Janet could see the blood trail until it reached the impacted snow that formed the outline of Akycha, and she realized that he'd fallen from the roof. This was when the puncture injury had likely occurred. As she took another step forward she felt a shortness of breath, it was as if she was winded, that something or someone had hit her so hard that the air had been drawn out of her body.

Janet gasped to refill her lungs, but she couldn't. Panic rose inside her body, she stepped back and felt the sensation of oxygen fill her lungs. The panic washed away, but she was confused. How is this possible? She pushed her body forward a little more, leaning this time rather than stepping and again the air had gone, or rather the oxygen she needed was gone, but she still felt the soft breeze. Janet took a few steps back and looked up at the roof remembering what John had said. He thought Akycha was suffering from acute mountain sickness, a condition that mountaineers suffer when climbing at high altitudes, but she felt even more confused at that possibility. How was it possible to suffer from AMS here? They were only 500 meters above sea level.

Concerned, not only at the worrying puzzle in front of her, but also by her own inability to come up with a logical explanation other than that of a weak Star Trek plot, she headed back toward the main building and the comfort of knowing John and Akycha were there. Even if Akycha was injured she felt that most basic of human emotions; safety in numbers. She entered the medical bay to find the two men as she'd left them. Akycha was now asleep, his blankets rising and dropping with his gentle breathing, and John still in the big chair reading. She whispered to him.

"John, come here." She beckoned him from the room.

John stood placing his book down, and made his way to the corridor where Janet now waited for him.

"What's up? You look worried."

"I've been to where Akycha had his accident."

"Can you tell what happened?" he asked.

"I Don't know where to start, I made it to the comms building, well most of the way. I stopped around three or four meters away, I was unable go any further, there seemed to be a barrier. Well I mean a...."

John had never seen her so agitated. One quality needed to work in such an environment as this was a cool head, the ability to work well under pressure and deal with life-or-death situations with a calm assuredness that would save lives, not cost them by fundamental errors in judgment.

"What is it?"

"When I got closer than three meters I felt the symptoms of AMS, which is what you said Akycha had when he first came into the hall."

"What?" John asked, puzzled.

Janet sighed and repeated what she'd just said. "When I got close to the comms building I had the effects of AMS, there was no, or little oxygen. I think Akycha felt these effects on the roof and fell off it trying to escape. The blood trail from his wound starts where he had impacted the ground, it's the only reasonable theory I can come up with."

John leaned against a window frame rubbing his forehead. He turned back to Janet at the same time pulling his sleeve up to check the time.

"Okay, let's not say anything just yet. I'll go back with Akycha in the chopper. You stay and take readings around the comms building. We'll file the report once we have a solid understanding of what happened."

"That's fine and good, but don't forget the first teams land in a week."

"I'll come back up tomorrow and help you with it, it shouldn't take too long. Whatever conditions made him fall from the roof appear to still be evident. Regardless, the evac chopper will be here soon. We'd better get our patient ready for transport."

Janet nodded as she looked over John's shoulder toward her sleeping friend. As she did the unmistakable sound of rotor blades cutting through the air came over the building as the chopper swung around to the helipad at the edge of the complex.

"About time!" John said. They turned and headed back into the medical room.

It was seconds later when the impact happened, shaking the building, causing dust to fall from the cracks and crevices it had gathered in. The lights flickered, some of them fell out if their mounting plates, hanging only by the wire that supplied the power to light them. Charts, memos and mission statements fluttered through the air lying amongst the dirt and dust that now covered the once clean floor.

A second impact came as Janet lay across Akycha, trying to protect him from falling debris. This time the lights, computers and monitors all failed; only the daylight from outside illuminated parts of the station. Windows this far north are considered a necessity for only parts of the station, too many windows leak too much heat, and compromise the structure of the building that the inhabitants rely on to keep them alive. Because of this design feature the station was in darkness, and the medical room was lit only by the small window John had leaned against only a few moments before. The glass in the window had shattered inward. Now light wasn't the only

147

thing that came through the gap where the glass had been, it was the bitter cold, and as the cold came in the heat escaped out.

As the building stopped shuddering, and a silence fell across them, Janet stood up from her protective position and looked at John.

"What was that?" she whispered

"I think it was the helicopter."

They both headed for the helipad. Outside was a scene from the latest and biggest disaster movie. Wreckage from the downed helicopter littered the once immaculate and virgin snow. The communication building now had a large wound to its north facing wall, and the dish that Akycha had just a short while before tried to re aligned now hung from its brackets by a charred and twisted cable. The array of aerials that used to run all of the stations communications, including the shortwave and CB, now lay across the crash site. They both realized that no communication would now be possible with Resolute. As they both stood looking around at the devastation, John broke the silence.

"Where is the fire?"

"What?" Janet answered him.

"The helicopter must have been carrying enough fuel for the return journey, so why is there no fire?"

"I don't...." Janet couldn't finish the sentence; she had no idea what to say.

"The same thing that brought the chopper down is the same thing you and Akycha experienced. It must be that, there is no other explanation. There is no oxygen!"

Janet stood speechless "But Akycha felt it on the roof of the comms building, I felt it two or three meters from the building. The chopper must have been three hundred feet up in his approach to the helipad."

"Then whatever is causing this is spreading. I think we should get a snow cat and leave."

"I'll get Akycha, you go get the transport cat. It's the only one we can get a stretcher in." Janet confirmed John's orders.

"Will do."

John nodded and headed back toward the main building, whilst Janet headed to the garages where only this morning she'd welcomed Akycha. Stepping forward cautiously, but with purpose, she felt the panic run around her body that maybe the next step she took would be a step into the vacuum she had felt earlier, and the vacuum that had brought down the helicopter.

She made it to the garage and the cat she needed to transport her two fellow passengers. Janet turned the key and the diesel engine fired up with a vibration she felt through her seat. With it came the sensation of relief they would soon be away from this place. Pulling down the gear stick into the D position, she sped up out and toward the main entrance.

As she rounded the corner she saw John standing with the stretcher by his side. As the cat pulled up John opened the side doors and pushed the stretcher inside and onto the readymade track system, locking the stretcher into place.

"Don't worry my friend, we'll soon be there," John reassured Akycha.

As he closed the door and made his way to the front passenger seat, the engine died. Janet turned the key, pumping the gas pedal at the same time.

"C'mon, c'mon you piece of shit!" She screamed as she tried to re-start the engine.

She looked across at John. When she did she saw a look of dread and alarm across his face, and she realized why. Her throat felt as if it was closing. She let go of the key and climbed out of the cat and headed toward John. As she did he recognized her actions and they met in front of the immobile vehicle.

John hugged Janet into him, both of them felt that with every exhale of carbon dioxide their lungs pushed out, the next inhale of oxygen became less and less until it became impossible to stand. They lowered themselves down leaning against the cat. Janet felt the warm realization wash over her. She was to die, in this place and in this moment. That she wouldn't get to fly home again at the end of this season, and that she wouldn't see her family and friends again and achieve her life's plans. She gasped pulling in what little oxygen she could, but soon it was hopeless.

There was no oxygen, her lungs tried hard, fighting against her own consciousness, it was now futile to try and breath. Panic had taken over, and anger at the thought that inevitable death was soon to follow. Adrenaline flooded her body, but she'd no use for this prehistoric response to mankind's early dangers. The only effect it had now was to cause her body to tremor and writhe. Nausea soon followed along with complete confusion and misperceptions. The writhing now gave way to convulsions which became ever more aggressive. She tried to reach for John, stretching her arms out, but she couldn't move. She looked at him, trying to find some help, some comfort, or even understanding. But John looked as terrified, and as confused as Janet felt. His eyes were blood shot and dilated. Blood ran from his nose and mouth as blood vessels burst, a sign his body was trying everything it could to maintain life, but with no oxygen it would be battle he would soon lose.

With one final and massive convulsion, John's neck snapped and his body became limp in front of her. The bright redness that had come over his face washed away into a ghostly white, and his twisted and contorted limbs lay limp and lifeless. Janet's vision now faded. The last thing she saw was the deep blue sky, and the last thing she thought of was the love for her mother and father.

Akycha had suffered the same fate. The vacuum that had started to envelop and circulate out from this place, like a predator stalking its prey had taken his life too. Strapped into the stretcher he'd slipped into unconsciousness and death during his medically induced sleep.

Part Three
The Anomaly
Goddard Flight Center

Chapter 9

In the former RHESSI control room, which had now become the headquarters for the President's action team (Investigation into Solar Anomalies and their Impact on Earth) or I.S.A.I.E, pronounced ISA for short, Jacob, Andy, Kevin and Alice watched on as Michael took a call from his superior in the White House.

"Yes sir, I understand, as soon as we find a working theory I will get back to you, thank you, sir. Goodbye." Michael ended the call. "Typical Monday morning," he said trying to break the silence that had come over them all when the phone had rung. "There has been some sort of incident in the north, in the Arctic Circle to be exact. A place called Axel Heiberg Island. Apparently, an emergency helicopter was sent to the McGill Artic Research Station, and when the helicopter didn't return a team was sent up. When they got there the helicopter had crashed and two bodies could be seen in front of a snow cat, but the locals claim they can't get too close because there is no oxygen."

"No air?" Jacob questioned his last statement.

Michael shrugged and repeated what he'd said "Seemingly, they can't get any closer than five meters to

154

the snow cat without oxygen masks. If they try, they can't breathe. They've managed to retrieve the bodies and post mortems have confirmed that they died from hypoxia. But here's the strange thing, while the doctor confirmed the cause of death, he was unable to explain how it happened."

"When did this happen?" Kevin asked.

"Two days ago." Michael answered and then continued. "The President wants us to be there tomorrow, and to make a start on this by the tenth, no later. So far, they've managed to keep it a secret. They've cancelled the first teams that were due to be landing there in a few days, and for now, the residents of Resolute don't suspect anything because the two people that run the station usually stay at the base during the season; a John Findley, and a Janet Woods, both now deceased."

"That's awful; do you think this is related to the event of last year?" Alice asked.

"I don't. What I do know is that we have two bodies in a morgue whose deaths can't be explained, a downed helicopter whose pilot is probably still amongst the wreckage, and so far, can't be retrieved, and a third member of the station's staff that can't be found." Michael answered.

The room became quiet again, and now Michael had the attention of everyone he continued.

"We leave tomorrow at seven a.m. The White House will have a plane standing by at Dulles airport, but not at the main terminal. It'll be out of sight of the commercial passengers. This is important, so listen carefully. Drive along Dulles Road then turn onto Rudder Road and finally Air Freight Lane. Park between the two hangars. There is a small runway that will be kept clear for us. These aerial maps are easy enough to follow. Any questions?" There was a silent pause. "Good, once on the aircraft we'll be taken to Resolute where we will spend the night. The following morning we'll be taken up to the research station, or as close as we can get to it. I'm going to hand each of you a list of the equipment we'll need, so I would suggest you finish up what you're doing and then return to your quarters to start packing."

With the office now quiet Michael sat at his station, making a list. As he did he heard the muted and whispered conversations between Kevin, Andrew and Jacob as they speculated on what they may find when they arrived on Wednesday. Michael didn't stop them, letting them speculate and make up scenarios would keep them occupied, and that in turn kept them from questioning him. But it didn't last as long as he would have liked.

"Has Bruce been notified of this field trip?" Jacob asked Michael.

"He was called separately at his home, and he'll be meeting us at the airport tomorrow morning."

After working tirelessly with the team to understand what had happened during the event and what could be done to prevent us being as vulnerable in the future, Bruce had taken two weeks' vacation to recharge. He, like the rest of the team, had assumed that there would be no surprises in the wake of the event.

Jacob nodded. "Are the list's ready?"

Michael handed Jacob a piece of white copy paper, he'd written the list on. "Remember we will need all of these items. The first three items you will find here; the remainder you will need to run into Washington for. I've been told that whatever I need to get to the bottom of this I can have, so if you have any difficulties let me know. I cannot over emphasize the importance of these items," Michael said.

Jacob took the sheet of paper from him and looked down at the list, wondering why he'd not written it on the computer and printed it. It was not like Michael to give people hand written, or in this case, hand scrawled lists. And besides, as it was not signed by Michael and it didn't bare his employer ID, he might have difficulty procuring the items. But he knew this was to avoid a paper trail until they'd discovered what had caused the unusual deaths, and what the consequences might or might not be.

Jacob nodded and looked back at the list to see what each item was.

1. *Torch & Batteries.*
2. *Cold weather Camping equipment.*
3. *Dehydrated food & power or energy bars.*
4. *Cold weather climbing clothing & boots (See Dan in stores, he'll be able to sort it all out today).*
5. *Paraffin heaters and portable stoves.*
6. *1x Shotgun 2x hand guns + ammunition.*
7. *Flair gun and six flares.*
8. *Iodine tablets & water purification equipment.*
9. *Plastic Whistle.*
10. *High altitude breathing gear. Eight sets. One each and two spare.*
11. *Acetazolamide and Dexamethasone (enough for each us for twice a day, for a week.)*

"You can come with me and help," Jacob said to Alice.

"Will do."

The following morning Michael arrived at the airport. Turning off Air Freight Lane he headed between the two large hangars. As he did, he could clearly see Bruce, Alice, Jacob, Andy and Kevin waiting patiently by the minivan they'd come in. Pulling his Range Rover into the adjacent parking spot, grabbing his gear from the trunk, he locked his car and joined the waiting crew.

"Hi Bruce." Michael greeted his friend. Though they'd known of each other before they'd been part of the team to deal with the magnetic storm, they had now become quite good friends, sharing similar tastes in music and entertainment, as well as hobbies and political views, and of course scientific views on the up-coming theories, such as string theory, and what there was before the Big Bang.

Bruce smiled back. "Hi Michael, last again."

As Michael came to rest at the back of the van by its open rear doors, he saw the boxes, bags and back-packs stacked almost to its roof. He turned to Jacob and the others. "Did you manage to get everything that was on the list?"

"Yes, we did." Alice answered.

"Okay then, let's get on the aircraft" Michael said rubbing his hands together.

They all helped pull the bags and boxes from the minivan, and load them onto the waiting trolley. Once empty, Andy locked it.

They headed over to the waiting plane. Michael had already identified it by the make, model, description and more importantly, the serial number which was written in large black letters along its fuselage, *QY-PBV*. The twin prop cargo plane easily swallowed the equipment they had brought. With it loaded the group of six climbed aboard. Jacob sat next to Alice.

"You ready?" he asked her.

Alice shrugged. "I don't know what to be ready for."

2500 miles and over eleven hours later, they were all happy to be able to leave the aircraft and walk off the stiffness and aching they felt. Jacob watched as Bruce and Michael arranged to have their luggage transferred to the waiting yellow bus, which had the words *Resolute Transport Solutions* written in blue on both sides.

He chuckled to himself, amused that no effort had been made to hide the fact that the vehicle that provided transport solutions was, in fact, an old-school bus. But he, like the rest of the group, was happy to sit in the more comfortable seats.

Jacob watched out of his window at the bleak surroundings he now found himself in as the old bus trundled its way along the only road that would take them to Resolute Bay. As the bus turned off Sun-Set Strip and onto a side road Jacob noticed was called, Dark Alley, it slowed and came to a stop outside a long plain looking building, mostly built of pre-fabrication. The large diesel engine of the bus became silent and with it the whistling flow of the warm air that they had embraced after the cold flight. Bruce stood at the front of the bus and addressed them, reminding Jacob of a teacher trying to get his pupils attention on the *once a year* school outing.

"Okay, this is the clinic where the two bodies are being stored. While we won't be examining them, we are meeting with the head of the rescue team that discovered them to try and get a picture of events before we travel to the site tomorrow. Any questions?".

Weary and tired from the days travelling Jacob hauled himself from his seat. The thick clothing necessary in these parts didn't make it any easier. Judging by the sighs and groans of Andy, Alice and Kevin, it seemed they had the same mind-set as Jacob. They climbed down from the bus onto the dirty blackened slush that was once white crisp snow. As they approached the main entrance the door opened and they were met by a tall, thin man. His trousers were thick lined ski dungarees, with braces that sat atop a thick woolen jumper.

His white hair and beard contrasted sharply against his skin which looked tanned and tight against his skull, as if all the moisture had been stripped away on a daily basis, which in these parts with wind chills in the winter months taking the temperature down to nearly −55 °C was not only possible, but quite common without the correct facial gear.

As Bruce approached him, the thin man held out his hand, and shook Bruce's. He gestured to the rest of them to make their way into the building. As Jacob entered, the man closed the door behind them. Following the others, Jacob headed through another open door and found himself in the building's meeting room. He had been in enough of these rooms to recognize it for what it was. At one end of the room hung a white screen with a projector hanging a few feet in front of it. On the adjacent table were two large stainless steel flasks, which had tea in one and coffee in the other and next to them, taking its rightful place, was a large jug of milk. Their host gestured to each of them to take one of the chairs which were uniformly laid out in a neat square block. Jacob sat on the end, perched ready for when they would be told to help themselves to a hot drink and biscuit.

The tall man stood at the front and began to speak.

"My name is Stephen Martin, and I'm a community administrator. Thanks for getting here on such short notice. I understand most of you are based in Washington DC and so I can imagine what a shock the change in climate and facilities are to you. Believe me, when I first arrived here I didn't see how I could stay for the two months I'd planned, but that was over thirty years ago. I'm sure Bruce and Michael have brought you up to date with what we found there and that we managed to retrieve two bodies."

Stephen paused. He looked around the room.

"What we found up there is still a mystery. It's akin to a cave man walking into a perfectly formed and polished window. He can touch it, and feel its interaction with him, and on him, but he can't see it or explain it. What we measured up there is accurate, but we have no idea how it has happened, how it can be, and how to halt it or what, if any the long-term effects the anomaly will have. But we do believe it has some collation with the event of last year. We know that it was in the southern hemisphere that the damage to the magnetosphere happened, and from that location M.A.R.S, the research station, is exactly at the opposite pole. Whatever that event was last year, I don't believe we've seen the last of the effects. To sum up gentlemen, we have stumbled upon what might be the most brilliant scientific find by mankind or the cradle of mankind's biggest nightmare. Tomorrow when you travel back to the research station I am hoping you can help us understand it."

Standing silent, Stephen looked at each of them. Jacob appreciated that Stephen wasn't as experienced with the event as the rest of them that sat in the room. But what he'd told them had chilled him more than any weather conditions outside. He looked across at Alice and she looked like she had when he'd first told her of the coming storm the previous year. "There are hot drinks at the back and some biscuits, help yourselves. I will hang around for any questions. And again, thank you all." The tall man finished.

The afternoon wore on. With the hot drinks finally gone along with the assorted biscuits, the group headed back outside to the waiting bus, while Bruce and Michael made the final arrangements to meet up with Stephen the following morning. Jacob settled back into his seat next to Alice on the bus. He was exhausted, and yet his mind raced trying to understand what had to be one of the strangest meetings he'd attended. By the time the bus had arrived at the only hotel in the town, Jacob was asleep. The warm air that once again flowed over him and the position he'd taken across the two seats had allowed his racing mind to slow down enough to permit him a little rest.

It was the sudden stop and jerking to a halt that all of these school buses did throughout his childhood that woke him, but it was the chitter chatter and banging of luggage that brought him to full consciousness.

"Nice sleep?" Alice asked as they waited in the narrow isle to exit the bus.

"Not really, no. I doubt I'll be able to sleep until we know what we're up against. I thought we were over the worst."

"We don't know yet that this is connected in any way to the event, it may just be a local phenomenon," Alice said.

"I hope so," Jacob answered.

Stepping from the bus, they made their way into the small hotel reception. Jacob made sure he was at the front of the group, desperate to get a key to the room he would call home for as long as they were here.

"You and Alice are sharing a room," Bruce said as Jacob took the key from the receptionist.

"What?" Jacob wasn't prepared. He knew they'd all grasped what was going on between Alice and himself, but to hear it said like that, and from his boss felt almost the same as it had when his mother had recognized that he was sharing a bed with his girlfriend when he was 18.

"Why, don't you want to?" Bruce asked.

"No, that's fine, I'm just a little surprised," Jacob said knowing he had to be careful what came out of his mouth next.

Alice took the key from him and picked up her luggage. "Smooth," she said as she led the way to their room.

It wasn't long before Jacob found himself where he wanted to be, laying on a soft mattress under thick blankets with his head buried deep in a soft pillow next to Alice. He watched the snow fall outside the triple-glazed windows as it passed through the light of the orange street lamps, and then disappeared back into the black of night. With the thoughts of what they might find tomorrow pushed deep to the back of his mind, he drifted into a deep and restful sleep.

The morning seemed to come around far too quickly for Jacob, but when he checked his phone it was indeed 7:45 a.m.; the time he'd set when he had gone to bed. But it felt like he'd only slept a few minutes, not nine hours. 'Fucking time always goes too fast when you want it to go slow.' He mumbled to himself as he watched Alice dress.

"How come we're in this room and we didn't, you know?"

Alice pulled up her trousers. "Because both of us were beat and you fell asleep as soon as your head hit that pillow," she answered.

"So, you would have?"

"Get dressed." Alice answered.

Jacob and Alice made their way to the breakfast room. Inside Kevin, Andy, Bruce and Michael sat eating.

"How's the breakfast?"

"Okay I guess, but I'll be glad to be home," Kevin replied.

"How did you sleep?" Andy asked, as he took a bite of his toast.

"I slept well but it seemed to pass by far too quickly," Jacob replied.

"Theory of Relativity," Andy replied swallowing his toast.

"I studied this and at no point did Einstein's Theory of Relativity mention sleep going by too quickly," Kevin said.

"Put you hand on a hot kettle, and a second seems to last an hour. Put you hand on a hot woman, and an hour seems to last a second." Andy explained.

"When he does have his hands on a hot woman he does only last a second," Alice said, poking fun at Jacob.

Kevin and Andy both laughed.

Bruce interrupted the jovial topic of conversation. "Right gentlemen, and lady, it is time to leave. Get your gear stowed in the truck and then get into the bus, if anybody wants a toilet or cigarette break you have ten minutes."

Andy pushed the remainder of his slice of toast into his mouth, chewing as he stood.

Kevin pointed at Andy and the mulched toast that rolled around on his tongue, breaking through his sealed lips to make a brief appearance.

"No wonder you're single with table habits like that,"

"Ah, but breakfast habits don't matter," Andy replied with both Kevin and Jacob knowing he was setting up another of his un-funny come backs.

"Oh, why is that?" Jacob knowingly took the bait.

"Because, breakfast comes after the night before, and by then I don't care what they think, because I've had what I wanted," Andy said.

"Yeah and that's the other reason your single," Alice said as they manhandled their gear onto the supply truck and then climbed aboard the bus. The journey from Resolute Bay to the research station was a long and thankless one. The scenery was bland to Jacob, mile after mile of white, and nothing to accompany them except the truck following diligently behind them.

"Any thoughts yet on you think this is?" Alice asked.

"None that make any sense," Jacob answered.

"What doesn't make sense may be the answer." Kevin joined in the conversation.

"What do you mean?" Alice asked.

"Sometime, when you're looking for answers in science, sometimes it's the things you believe don't exist or make sense, that end up being the answer." Jacob explained.

"Theoretical physicists use it constantly," Kevin said.

"Stephen said there seemed to be no oxygen, there are places on earth where there is no oxygen, such as the Dead Sea or even the Atlantic White Cedar Swamps found along the eastern coast of the U.S. These *dead zones* can exist because of chemical or physical conditions. But they have one thing in common. They are bodies of water. There is no place on earth where oxygen is absent in the air," Jacob said.

"What does that mean?" she asked.

"The only thing in nature that matches what he told us is a vacuum. But that isn't possible on a planet like ours which has an atmosphere."

The bus came to a stop with another jolt. Jacob, Alice, Kevin and Andy saw that they had arrived at the research station. Out of his window Jacob could see the exact image of the photos that had been included in the file. In the foreground was the yellow snow cat, and behind it the main entrance to the station with the doors still wide open.

As he stepped off the bus he saw that they had parked around fifteen meters in front of the bright red boundary tape marker that the original team had used to mark the edge of the *No oxygen barrier*. Bruce gathered them in a circular group around himself and Michael.

"Okay everyone. We have parked a little farther away than the first team. From here we will deploy the small robot fitted with the air oxygen sensor array and see if this barrier has increased or retreated. Are we all clear?" Bruce said.

"Why is there no fresh snow on the cat or the boundary tape, or even the buildings?" Jacob asked.

Bruce looked puzzled "How do you mean?"

"Last night I watched snow fall outside our hotel. And we're standing in fresh powder. Look at the tracks the bus made."

The others looked at the tracks.

Jacob continued. "But there is no fresh snow on the snow cat or the buildings, and tracks made when they dragged the bodies out from the front of the snow cat are still fresh. Hell, they haven't even been covered by any wind blowing snow over them."

Bruce looked at Jacob.

"Well that is why we're all here. Isn't it?"

Chapter 10
McGill Artic Research Station.
North Pole

February 9th, 2023.

Kevin was at the controls of the small tracked robot, officially called the *Mars All Terrain Independent Scout,* but affectionately called MATIS for short. The robot was used on earth's many differing terrains after NASA had abandoned its use on the SOL 1 mission in favor of a larger and much more complicated robot, which also had the advantage of *self-driving-awareness,* which meant it could be let go without the need for remote piloting. MATIS trundled past Kevin, Andrew and Jacob toward the boundary tape. Its on-board sensors had been altered to measure air pressure and oxygen levels, as well as other trace elements and gases such as sulphur dioxide, carbon dioxide and carbon monoxide. The information was then wirelessly transferred via a local network to a bank of four laptops.

Their base and accommodation for the next twenty-four hours was a large artic survival tent which was specially designed to withstand the temperatures and weather conditions which were typical for this region. The entrance to the tent was through an airlock which ensured that whatever the weather was outside, it would not be able to breach the interior. Once inside, the tent consisted of a large communal area. This was where the team would cook, eat and carry out the investigation, and it was where the laptops were set up. At the back and sides of the tent were seven pods that jutted out from the main area which provided six bedrooms and one bathroom with a chemical toilet. The tent was powered by a small generator and solar panel.

Sat at the table where the laptops were situated was Kevin. In front of him was a screen which displayed the view from the HD camera fitted to MATIS. Bruce, Michael, Andy, Jacob and Alice were sat around him watching the video feed and the data relayed back by the sensors.

"Now be careful." Andy goaded Kevin as he carefully pushed the small joystick forward on the remote controller.

"Watch what you're doing. Don't hit the snowcat." Jacob laughed joining in.

"Will you two fuck off," Kevin said trying his hardest not to laugh with them.

When MATIS reached a distance of two meters before the tape, the first alarm sounded.

"Stop!" Bruce shouted on hearing the alarm.

Kevin released the joystick and the robot came to an abrupt stop.

"What's the alarm for?" Bruce turned to Michael who was monitoring the readouts inside the tent.

Michael's eyes went immediately to monitor three, the one sounding the alarm. Red writing flashed across the screen, covering the data. Michael hit the escape button on the laptop and the warning disappeared, revealing the data which had caused the alarm to sound. Michael studied the information, then removed his glasses and rubbed his eyes before looking at it again. The look on his face reflected the disturbing information.

"What is it?" Bruce asked.

"See for yourself," Michael replied, standing back and pointing his glasses at the screen, allowing Bruce a closer look.

"This isn't correct. It can't be," Bruce said.

Hearing the conversation Andy and Jacob crowded around the seventeen-inch flat screen. They could see for themselves what had alarmed Michael and Bruce.

MATIS had detected a drop, in oxygen levels. They had received the reports of there being no oxygen, but they'd assumed the first team that filed them had miss-read their instruments. Within nature a vacuum couldn't exist on any planetary body that had an atmosphere, regardless of what the atmosphere consisted of. But MATIS, which had the latest technology, was telling them just that. But there was something else. The first team had erected the tape where they had insisted all oxygen was void. But MATIS had sounded its alarms two meters before that boundary. Either the first team had placed the tape wrongly or the boundary was expanding.

Jacob was the first to speak. "This can't be correct; there must be something wrong with the sensor."

"It was calibrated this morning before the robot was deployed." Kevin answered him.

Bruce had put Kevin in charge of MATIS before they'd arrived, only because of Kevin's previous work with NASA and robotics. Albeit, it was a short posting, he was still clearly the most qualified in this small team to handle the delicate nature of these smaller expeditionary robots. Kevin now felt that any insult or slur aimed at MATIS was a direct slur at him, and that wasn't something that sat well with him.

Bruce broke the silence. "Let's see what happens if we back it up. If the alarm keeps sounding, we know it's the sensor. If not, we'll know the sensor is good, even if that means facing up to what it's telling us should not be possible. At least not here."

Kevin lifted the controller, which now hung loosely around his neck supported by a thin nylon lanyard. Slowly he pulled the joystick backwards. The robot responded and moved back along the tracks it had made in the snow. It had only moved its own length before the warnings, and readings on the laptop that had startled them disappeared, and all the readings became normal again.

"Stop!" Michael shouted and the robot halted.

Picking up one of the many small red flags they had brought with them, Michael exited the tent and walked to the front of the robot and planted the flag adjacent to its left caterpillar track. After making sure it was planted in the tightly packed snow, he unclipped his walkie talkie and spoke to Kevin.

"Okay Kevin. Forward again, slow as you can please."

Kevin pushed the small trimming button forward which was used for minute adjustments and for crawling speeds, precisely the speed Michael had just requested. The robot started slowly forward, passing once again through its own tracks and past the red flag, and as before, laptop three started its alarm and flashing red writing came on the screen. This time it was ignored.

"Keep going," instructed Michael.

The little robot reached the end of its tracks and pushed ahead through the newly laid flat crisp virgin snow. As it reached the boundary tape, the second alarm sounded on laptop one. As it did the robot moved off the new snow and was now travelling on the older snow Jacob had pointed out to them on their arrival. Kevin, unsure now what he should do, looked over at Bruce for guidance, who waved his hand in a gesture that meant continue forward. As the robot passed under the tape, laptop two sounded its alarm.

"Stop it there Kevin, I'm coming back to the tent."

Kevin pulled back the trim wheel and the robot slowed to a gentle stop, waiting patiently for its next command. Michael came back in and they all gathered around the laptops, three screens now showed the flashing writing and sounded their alarms. One by one they were each muted before the information was studied and deciphered in as much detail as they could with the short time they had, while wanting to finish the robot's circulation of the base in one day. As with the first laptop, the data they were seeing should not be possible, here or anywhere else on earth. But one laptop remained. The laptop that was fitted with arguably the most important sensor was still silent.

"Can you make it to the snowcat?" Michael asked.

"If I stand by the red flag you planted to mark the boundary of the first alarm, I may have the range."

Michael nodded. "Okay, try it."

Kevin left the tent and made his way to the red flag that stood out against the brilliant white snow. As Bruce, Michael, Andy, Alice and Jacob followed him, Kevin pushed the joystick forward and MATIS responded, pushing its way through and over the previously flattened snow and the larger tracks the snowcat had made on its fateful journey from the garage to the station entrance, just a few days before.

As it did laptop 4 finally sounded its alarm, and in the empty tent red writing filled its screen, but none of them moved, each of them stared at the little robot as it finally reached the snowcat.

"Hold it there." Michael instructed him.

Kevin nodded and put the joystick back to its natural position and the robot stopped by the open side door of the snowcat. Michael turned first and the others followed as he headed back to the tent. Once inside they read the data that the screen of laptop 4 displayed with a sense for foreboding.

It was as if they knew what it would say; they had guessed by the readings on laptops one, two and three what the sensors on laptop four would tell them. But none of them had confirmed it in their own minds; they had each of them devised a way of making what they'd been told to also be impossible. But now it was confirmed. Now there would be no alternative outcomes or denying of the facts, and there may be no other possible scenarios. A vacuum had formed around the research center. And all of the indications showed that it was growing.

The data they had was enough to leave this place and present their findings to the President. They knew this should happen with a sense of urgency, but they also understood that they didn't have all the answers yet, they had to stay and complete the other task that they'd come here to do. Michael moved his attention from the laptop which had hailed the inescapable and ominous readings to the smaller screen which was linked to the HD camera on MATIS.

"How high can this camera reach Kevin?" Michael broke the silence and the others joined him by the screen, which was split into four equal segments, each designated with the camera whose view they showed.

"What's your thinking Michael?" Kevin asked.

"I want to look inside the snowcat, see if there any clues in there."

"Camera one is fixed, camera two is night vision and three is a FLIR. If you want to look inside, Camera four is on an extendable mount."

"How high can it rise?" Michael asked again.

"Well, the robot stands four feet, and the mount extends around another four feet, so it will be able to see into the Cat."

"Okay, go do it."

Kevin moved back outside and towards the flag. He pushed a little green button that sat on top of the remote that had been designated for Camera four. Slowly, the mount extended up and forward, rising at a slant. It reached the half-way point of its range when Kevin heard "STOP!"

Kevin released the button and returned to the tent. The image sent back by camera four clearly showed the body of Akycha, lying where Janet and John had left him on the day they'd all perished.

Solemnly, Bruce spoke. "It would appear we have found the missing team member."

"Why didn't the first team take his body with the other two?" Alice asked.

"I can only assume they didn't look in the cat; they must have thought he was in the helicopter." Bruce answered.

"It could also be that the apparatus they had wouldn't have given them enough time to look around. Bio hazard and oxygen suits are only suitable in an atmosphere. In a vacuum, they wouldn't provide protection for more than a few minutes," Jacob said.

A silence fell among them. It had been a day of impossible findings, which had left each of them emptied and beaten.

"Kevin bring the robot away from the snowcat and to this side of the tape, but leave the sensors running over night, we'll see if there are any changes. As for the rest of us I think we should call it a day. I for one have seen enough."

Kevin moved MATIS to where Bruce had instructed him and put its sensors and cameras on auto mode, a feature that was left over from the days when it was destined for Mars exploration. But it was doubtful that if it had made it to the red planet it would have unwittingly played the important role in human history that it had done today. The others secured the tent airlock and entrance to keep out the freezing temperatures the coming night would certainly bring, and moved back to the living compartment where they settled down to eat yet another high calorie, but cardboard tasting field ration.

"You know when we were told that the first team had stated there was no oxygen I didn't believe them," Andy said.

"No, me neither. I assumed they'd become muddled up somehow," Bruce said.

"There's no doubt now. It's not just that there's no oxygen, it's the fact that a vacuum has formed around the research station. How is that even possible?" Jacob said.

"I don't know. But we have all the information we can collect. Tomorrow we'll pack up and head home and present our findings."

"And then what?" Alice asked.

"Then we'll have to find a way to repair whatever is causing this," Bruce said.

"And if it can't be repaired. If it can't be stopped?"

"Then I'm sure the White House has procedures in place to deal with it."

"You know as well as I do that's horse shit Bruce," Michael said.

"Do I?" Bruce scoffed.

"There are no procedures to deal with a vacuum on earth. And you know why? Because up until today it wasn't thought possible that one could exist. To answer your question Alice, if it can't be repaired. Then we don't have a fucking clue what to do."

"Do you think it's connected to the event of last year?" Alice asked.

"It has to be, as the damage to the earth's magnetosphere happened in the southern hemisphere, on the exact opposite pole to where we are now. It's too much of a coincidence for there not to be a connection," Andy said.

"Ok, what's the plan when we meet with the President's scientific advisers?" Andy asked Bruce.

"The first thing we need to do is look at the southern hemisphere. See if there's a correlation to what we're seeing here. Confirm it once and for all."

"An early start then?" Kevin asked.

Bruce yawned. "Yeah."

They turned in, but all of them had trouble sleeping. Perhaps because of the thoughts they all had. Thinking about the day's findings, or perhaps to think about what today's findings meant for them, their loved ones, their friends, or even for us all.

February 10th, 2023. Base camp tent.

Jacob woke first as it always seemed to be. While he bitched about it to the others he secretly preferred the early mornings this way. He slipped out of the bed trying not to wake Alice who as usual was still in a deep sleep. Until the others woke he would have the accommodation section to himself, though it was small, for the remaining time they would be here it would have to do. The only alternative was the bus, but any survival expert worth their fee will tell you that sleeping in a vehicle is one of the quickest ways of inviting death.

For Jacob, this morning routine suited him; he would have fresh coffee and the peace and quiet he needed to start the day. Pulling open the flap that formed his bedroom door, he stepped out and headed for the stove and the coffee machine. Weary and somewhat bleary eyed he filled the jug with water and placed a generous portion of coffee in the filter. He flicked the *on* button and leaned against the counter. He yawned rubbing his eyes desperately, trying to get them to catch up with the rest of him.

It was then he noticed the laptop screens and more importantly, what they were displaying. That sickening sense of dread and adrenalin started to wash over him, as it quickly dawned on him that the alarms had not been reset after they were muted the previous day, and though he knew what the flashing red writing on the screens meant, the fact that the warnings had been trigged overnight, now meant that this anomaly was now much closer to them, and had passed the red flag.

His mind scrambled as he tried to bring it to full consciousness. He started to shout the others. If the laptops had failed to raise an audible alarm, then Jacob would do it himself.

"GET UP! EVERYONE GET UP!" He shouted as loud as his morning lungs allowed.

Running back to the bedroom compartments, he shook the thin nylon flaps as he continued to raise the alarm.

"Jesus, get up. It's moved, it *has* grown."

Michael was the first to emerge.

"What the fuck is the noise about?"

"Look at the monitors, look at them, everyone is flashing! Every God damn one," Jacob answered, his lungs now depleted and his throat sore.

Jacob followed Michael towards the bench, though both of them walked carefully, they couldn't tell where the boundary was they only knew it had moved during the night. They reached the monitors as the rest joined them, everyone asking at once what the commotion was and all becoming silent when they saw the screens flashing their red warnings. Stunned and still not fully awake, Bruce sat down in front of the fourth monitor. Kevin and Andrew stood still, rooted to the spot where they'd first seen the monitors.

Michael spoke first. "Kevin, can you use the cameras on the robot to bring it back towards the tent?"

"Err, yes, yes I can. I can do that from here the range should be okay." Kevin stuttered at first, his mind seemed to forget its own filing system. For one second he was unable to think clearly. But his thoughts came back.

Kevin picked up the remote and pressed the little green button once again. Camera four came to life with a flicker of static before an image of snow and the red flag came on the screen. Carefully, Kevin turned MATIS around. He didn't dare allow it to snag a caterpillar track, not now. To his private relief, it didn't. Kevin now moved the robot towards them. As the robot continued to push through the snow, the alarms continued flashing. MATIS now moved within the boundary of long guide ropes of the tent, but still all four monitors showed their ominous warnings. Kevin looked around the group, all of them focused intently between the bird's eye view of MATIS and the four laptop screens.

Keeping the joystick pushed forward the red flashing remained. How the hell can this be? Kevin thought to himself, sweat now running down his back as beads of it collected on his forehead.

MATIS, now only its own length from the entrance kept coming and still the red warnings flashed, and then nothing. All four screens went back to show a normal state. Almost in perfect unison the group let out a sigh. Kevin was still as tense as he had been since he first saw the monitors. He followed the little robot's path until the camera screen had gone black at the exact point the warnings had cleared, but the others hadn't noticed, not yet.

Only Kevin understood why the screen had gone black. It was because the camera lens was now pushed tightly against the tents entrance flap to its airlock. The Boundary had moved to the edge of their tent. Kevin backed the robot away from the tent and within one body length of itself, the alarms sounded and flashed again. Bruce turned to Kevin, not understating why they'd come back across the screen but he could see by his ashen expression it wasn't good. He watched as Kevin pushed the joystick forward and then followed his line of sight. On the view screen, they all saw that MATIS was inside the airlock. Bruce immediately understood why Kevin wore the expression that he did, he turned and alerted the others who still seemed oblivious to the danger they were in.

"Oh God, the Robot is in the airlock, the boundary to this anomaly has moved during the night, and it's in here. With us," Bruce said.

Michael reacted and turned to Kevin. "If we bring the robot inside the tent, park it in the middle, dead center, and keep the sensors running. How long will the batteries last?"

"They have a run time of around seventy-two hours, but I can plug it in to the power supply that the laptops are using. Then it'll be good until and generator runs dry plus the seventy-two hours."

"That's it! I'm calling a halt to this investigation we have what we came for. We'll leave the tent up and the robot connected to the laptops. Jacob, can you set up a satellite link, so we can receive the data from the robot in our control room?"

Jacob nodded, still stunned and alarmed at the distance the boundary had moved in a single night, but he was now also relieved that Michael had called it and was pulling them back to where he liked to be. Home.

"Jacob?" Michael snapped at him, missing Jacobs subtle head nodding "You'll do that yes?"

"Yes Michael, I'll sort it now." Jacob started to configure the network to report directly to the main frame at the former RHESSI control room. With a final click of the mouse, the darkened screens inside the darkened control room they had left only a few days ago lit up displaying the same readings as the laptops in front of them. Jacob's final act was to lock the laptops to their log-in screens, making sure that if someone did venture inside after they'd left, no data would be seen.

Michael watched as Kevin maneuvered the robot to the middle of the tent. Then he pulled out its external power cord and plugged it directly in the main power supply from the generator.

Michael started his announcement again. "Listen up, we have no idea how fast this boundary is moving, or in which direction until we study the data that is now being transmitted back to head-quarters. The main thing now is our safety. The suits and oxygen gear we brought will not keep us protected once we pass the boundary and into this anomaly, they're not designed to work within a vacuum. Finding the helicopter and its pilot is off the agenda. We need to leave this area; in fact, we need to evacuate. Get what you need to travel and the kit we're taking back and be on the bus within five minutes."

"What about the boundary movement? I can't imagine Stephen would be very happy about leaving here without some warnings, or predictions," Andy asked Michael.

"Don't worry. Once back at the hotel I'll go to the *RCMP* station and report what we have found, and tell them to keep it closely monitored. Bruce, can you get hold of the pilot, tell him to be ready to leave in three hours?"

"Three hours? I'm not sure we can be ready that quickly." Bruce questioned the time limit Michael had ordered.

"I know it sounds tight, but here's the thing. We have found what we came for. We know what killed the research station's staff, and we found the third member of the team. But we've also found that this, this anomaly, or whatever you want to call it, this thing, that according to all the laws of physics as we understand them, shouldn't be here, is. More than that, more than all of that, it's expanding, it's growing. I for one know that we need to get back to Washington. We need to inform the White House and work on a resolution," Michael said.

Now it was clear to all of them that if this thing continued to expand, the consequences to the planet, to mankind, and to all life would be catastrophic. It would be like nothing the world had witnessed, and that included the time the earth changed from just another rock spinning through space to the time the first microscopic bacteria flickered into life in the primeval ooze from which all life on earth came.

Quietly and efficiently, they cleared the tent of the equipment and belongings they needed. With the bus, less full than when they arrived, the crew boarded, Kevin took one last look inside the tent and its lone remaining team member MATIS. He checked again the status of its systems and placed a hand on it. "See ya buddy," he said affectionately. Kevin had enjoyed his time working in the robotics department at NASA. He always saw them as more than the collection of wires and circuitry they were. And with MATIS it was no different. This sentry would stand alone and relay information back to their headquarters. And for that Kevin was grateful. He left the tent by the rear emergency access, securing it behind him, he climbed aboard the bus for the journey back to Resolute.

Once they had arrived they disembarked and headed inside the hotel. Michael drove on to the RCMP office to file his report, warning the police that no one should go to the research station for any reason.

10th February 2023.

Flight back to Dulles International Airport

Jacob looked at the view from his window seat. At thirty thousand feet, it was high enough to see over a wide area, but low enough to make out land marks and details. He looked forward to the front of the fuselage. Kevin and Andy sat a few rows in front of him, sharing a private conversation.

A few rows ahead of them sat Bruce and Michael. It seemed their conversation wasn't quite as private, or it had occurred to them that the noise of aircraft was loud enough to drown out their voices from anyone trying to listen, making Jacob think that the same logic hadn't occurred to Kevin and Andy. He looked to his left and to where Alice was sat, she was busy writing. He thought of disturbing her but decided against it. Instead he put on his headphones and listened to music.

Finally, he thought as the plane touched down and taxied to where they'd first boarded. They were all eager to get off. But before any of them had a chance to head for the exits Bruce and Michael stood at the front of the plane and addressed them.

"Okay, listen up. Before we all split and head home I've been in contact with the President's scientific adviser. We're meeting with him tomorrow. Given the serious nature and sensitivity of what we found up there, they have invited us to stay in Washington DC tonight under protection. They've sent a minivan for us and until it arrives we are not allowed to leave the plane, so I suggest you all just sit tight," Bruce said.

"Oh, come on, we have got lives beyond our work. Can we not just meet them there tomorrow? It's not like it's a long drive." Kevin protested.

"When I say we've been invited, what I mean is we've been ordered, so it doesn't matter how much you whine and bitch about it, it's a done thing. So, I would suggest you make the best of it," Bruce replied.

Kevin, Andy, Alice and Jacob looked between each other with the same look of defeat.

"Well at least it's not cold and it's not a tent again," Alice said, offering some comfort.

Chapter 11
Outside the Oval Office: The White House, Washington DC.

February 11th, 2023: 9:45 a.m.

Jacob had never felt more uncomfortable and that he didn't belong in a situation than the one he found himself in now. In just a few minutes he would be speaking directly to the President of the United States. Alice had stayed back at the Goddard Flight Center, along with Kevin and Andy who had stayed up overnight to collect and collate the information MATIS was sending back. Bruce, Michael and Jacob needed the information to be as up to date as possible, and even now Bruce was receiving updates from Kevin. Michael was talking to Jonathan Moore, the lead scientific advisor to the White House within this President's administration. It was Jonathan that had requested the team go to Resolute, and arranged for them to meet with the President today to present their findings.

After a few minutes, they were asked to take a seat in the Oval Office and wait for the President. The Oval Office looked as it had in the movies Jacob had watched; two couches opposite each other with a low table between them, and the President's desk dominating the room. Sitting opposite Bruce and Michael on the low couches with Jonathan next to him, Jacob looked around the room. They were surrounded by four large men in dark suits who stood by each of the room's doors. Of course, each man had a curly wire visibly from their right ear.

"This is nerve wracking." Jacob whispered to Jonathan.

Johnathan tried to assure him. "Just remember, stay calm and answer directly and truthfully."

One of the secret service men touched his right ear and then spoke into his jacket sleeve.

"Roger that, Potus on the way. Over."

Jacob looked at his nervous co-workers who acknowledged what they'd just heard. One of the heavy doors opened and the President walked through it. Behind him walked two more men: one in a smart suit and one wearing army dress uniform. Jacob's observations and day dreaming were stopped abruptly by a tap on his shoulder from Jonathan as he attempted to get Jacob's attention to join them as they stood to welcome the President. Standing 6'4" and with a frame to match his height the President greeted his visitors.

The man in the smart suit spoke first. "Gentlemen please let me introduce President Benjamin Young." Jacob surmised this was the President's aid.

"Good morning and welcome back to Washington," the President said.

"Mr President, let me introduce some of the team that travelled to Resolute, and who are working on the ISA project. This is Bruce McCaughey, formally head of the Martialis Project, next to him is Michael Forbes, formally the head of RHESSI, and this is Jacob Miller," Jonathan said.

President Young welcomed them and then sat behind his desk. "I understand you have rushed back to present your conclusions to my team. Is that correct?" he asked Bruce.

"Yes, that's correct, Mr President."

"I've read the brief you sent to Jonathan last night, and as I understand it you believe there is a vacuum developing which you also state is increasing in size. Please elaborate on the report and what we can do to fix it," President Young said.

Bruce cleared his throat. "We were sent up there by Jonathan because an unusual event had happened. Two scientists died in a suspicious way. They had suffocated and by the way their bodies presented it would be correct to say that they were put into a vacuum, but of course that would be ludicrous as the only place we know we can create a vacuum on earth is at the NASA training complex, designed and built to train astronauts on the effects of being in a vacuum whilst in their space suits." Bruce answered.

"Is that what the original report said, Jonathan?" President Young asked.

"It said the scientists had died from asphyxiation, but the only places on earth that have no oxygen at all are in bodies of water, not on land, and because of the location I felt we needed a clear explanation." Jonathan answered.

"And it's correct that the location where this happened is the polar opposite of where the magnetosphere was damaged by SOL 1 last year?" President Young asked.

"Yes sir," Jacob answered.

"According to the laws of physics, as we know them, it should be impossible for a vacuum to be created and exist on earth, which has an atmosphere that supports a planet size eco-system with diverse species, everything from single-cell amoebae to what we believe to be the most complex living organism that has ever walked this planet or existed in the universe, which is of course mankind," Michael said.

"But you're saying one *has* been created?" President Young asked.

"Let's not forget that no matter how magnificent the earth is it is also extremely vulnerable. The damage SOL 1 inflicted showed that clearly. For a while now we have concluded that Mars once supported an eco-system much like our own, but because it is much smaller than earth, its magnetosphere could not protect it against solar storms. Eventually the planet was stripped to what we see today. The more we study Mars, the more this thesis appears to be true," Jonathan said.

"What are you saying?" The President asked him directly.

"What I am saying is that there is a vacuum which has formed over the research facility in Resolute, and that vacuum did kill the management team. We now believe what happened on Mars, Mr President, an eon ago, has started happening here on earth. And like Mars, we see no way that this anomaly, this vacuum, call it what you will, but we see no evidence why it will rectify itself, in fact quite the opposite. While we were there it increased in size," Bruce said.

"If this is true gentlemen, what is the long-term prognosis?" President Young asked Jonathan.

"We don't know, Mr President. Bruce and his team had measured an overall area of forty thousand square meters while they were there. They have left a robot fitted with the necessary instrumentation. Since then we've been monitoring those reading through the night, and we're continuing to do so, which is why the other team members aren't here. It is continuing to grow at around seven square meters every twelve hours. However, to make an accurate estimate we would have to fly over it. But the last guy who tried was the helicopter rescue unit and it didn't end well for him, no air, no combustion, meaning no engine and no lift."

"There is one solution," Jacob said.

"What would that be?" President Young asked.

"A drone, we could send one over the area affected in Resolute and one over the southern pole," he answered.

"I read in the brief you believe it's the southern pole that's damaged?" President Young asked Bruce.

"Yes sir, it would support why it's the northern hemisphere that's showing the first signs of this anomaly."

"I'm not sure I follow," President Young said.

"If you tip a glass of water upside down the water at the bottom of the glass is the last to drain, that's what we believe is happening here. If the atmosphere has a hole at the South Pole, the effects would be felt first on the polar opposite location, which is Resolute," Jonathan said.

"NASA?" Jacob said out loud, surprising himself.

"What?" asked the President.

Jacob squirmed a little, realizing that all eyes were on him. "NASA has a drone program. They thought if they could somehow make them work on another planet or the moon, they would put together a preliminary chronicling of any area which would quicken the decision where to put the robots. They took a few first generations from the army when they replaced them and retro-fitted them with environmental instruments. It would be a quick process to make the exact changes we'd need."

"Make it happen, Jonathan," President Young said. The he turned to Bruce. "Bruce, you still haven't laid out what you think the outcome of this will be."

Bruce looked among his team first, and to Jonathan for guidance in the way he should answer, and each of them seemed to say to him *spell it out.* He took a deep breath, shaking with nerves and with the thoughts that had troubled him since he'd worked out what the inevitable outcome would be flowing freely around his mind, he pulled his strength and resolve back and turned to face the President.

"Mr President. I believe that unstopped this anomaly will continue to grow until it has enveloped our planet and all life on earth has ceased to exist, nothing on earth can survive in a vacuum."

Bruce clamped his hands together. Sweating, he took a deep sigh before reaching for the glass of iced water which was placed on the table in front of him and took a big gulp, as he pulled open his tie and shirt button. He had just told the President the world was going to end, not in a trillion years or even forty million years when our sun eventually dies, but that it would end in their lifetime.

The Oval Office once again became silent as they tried to understand the magnitude of what that one sentence meant for mankind and for all life on earth. Now it was time for the represented armed forces to speak. It was the man who'd remained silent throughout this meeting and who wore the dress uniform that spoke next: General Scott.

"With permission, Mr President?" He started and then aimed his question at Bruce. "You said that this anomaly would eventually envelop the planet, but there must be something we can do, something that our technology can do?"

"I haven't thought of anything yet. Our technology will count for nothing when this starts to spread, unless you want to dress all of mankind in astronaut's suits. But then of course that means we would just starve to death because all other life will be dead." Bruce answered the General as directly as he could, without seeming disrespectful, but the General hadn't finished.

"Well. I am sorry son but, can't and nothing we can do, have never been in my dictionary. We can go into space. Hell! We have people on Mars right this minute and people at the bottom of sea," General Scott answered.

"I understand that General, but there are over seven billion people living on this planet. Everyone, no matter where we live, relies on a fragile and delicate balance which starts with the smallest bacteria, to the rotation of the sun and even the angle at which the earth orbits it. Sending people into space or to the bottom of the sea is easy, but saving an entire planet is something different."

"Hell, I didn't mean the whole planet son."

"What do you mean?" Bruce asked.

"I meant saving the people who need to be saved; those people that need to restart civilization, to run governments, scientists, and the military."

"Believe me General. It won't matter who you are, who you know, who your connections are or how rich you are. As it has been throughout history, death doesn't discriminate. If we can't stop this no one will survive. It would be the end," Jonathan said.

"With respect General, they're right and we're off topic. Jonathan, arrange a drone for Bruce's deployment. Under Presidential order, every project NASA is currently involved with ceases immediately apart from the Martialis mission of course, and all their attention is turned to this. Budget does not matter. What does matter gentlemen, is security. If this was to leak into the public domain, what will follow will be a complete breakdown of all social order and rules. The whole system that has kept mankind separate from the animals and our own primeval instincts will collapse, and then it won't matter about a vacuum. Mankind will annihilate itself." The President took a deep breath, sighed and turned to Bruce. "Once you have the data from the drone, how long will it take you to compile the data into an accurate and useful count down? A time scale if you will?"

Bruce paused before he answered him. "I think we can bring together the data and have a time scale within twelve hours, but please remember Mr President, it may not be one hundred percent accurate. There are a lot of variables that haven't been used in this way before, after all, this will be the first time we have worked with information like this."

"Just do your best Bruce, that's all I can ask."

"We will Mr President. I'll work with Jonathan on the drone."

"Thank you, Bruce. Now if that's all?"

Bruce, Michael and Jacob stood to leave, but were halted by one last remark from the President.

"It goes without saying gentlemen that this is official and top secret. Any passing on of what you know of this or the discussion today will be treated as treason and punished accordingly."

With that warning ringing in their ears, they left the oval office with Jonathan and the President's aid, and as they left, President Young dismissed his security.

With the office door shut President Young turned to General Scott. "Make arrangements to have them checked and followed with everything, texts, calls, internet activity and personal conversations. We cannot risk this becoming known to anyone, do you understand? They must *not* cross the line."

"I do Mr President, and what should we do if one of them does?"

President Young looked around the room and then back to General Scott.

"You get them to remain silent, how is up to you."

"There is one other thing sir," General Scott said.

"Yes. Martialis," the President said.

"If the real motives behind the SOL 1 mission, and our urgency to beat the other nations to Mars were made public, the consequences would be catastrophic," General Scott said.

"Then make sure it doesn't come out," President Young warned him.

General Scott left the office leaving the President alone to fully absorb and understand the surreal conversation he'd just been a part of. As he looked at the portraits that hung around the room of past Presidents, who history would always remember for the good they did for mankind, and for making the United States a superpower and the country of opportunity and dreams for anyone of any creed and color, he wondered what they would have done. But he also wondered what he should now do. After all, he was not now destined to be the President that would be remembered for great feats of wisdom and humanity, helping those in his own country and countries around the world fight discrimination and tyrants. No, if this can't be stopped, and history was to be recorded at all, he would be remembered as the President that watched over the demise of mankind and the death of the earth.

February 12th, 2023. 11:38 a.m.
Goddard Space Center. ISA control parking lot

Bruce watched as the large semi-truck pulled up, its air breaks hissing as it did. The large white truck which had the NASA logo on the side of its trailer housed the flight control for the drones they would deploy over both Resolute, and over Antarctica, 70°55'37.3"S 74°41'58.3"E, the polar opposite position to Resolute and the exact point where the engines of SOL 1 had the largest effect on the magnetosphere.

The drones themselves would be launched from facilities closer to the coordinates they would fly over. Though they could be piloted from anywhere in the world using the surviving military satellites they still had fuel limitations. Any data they collected would be sent back directly to the ISA control room.

The NASA pilots who had been seconded from the U.S. Airforce knew where their flight paths would take them, but they had been told it was purely a training run to see if two drones could withstand the temperatures and if the base technology could receive and decipher information simultaneously when sent from opposite sides of the planet. But it would be another forty-eight hours before both drones would be ready for their flight. The first drone was currently being flown to Resolute Bay Airport on a U.S. military transport; the Canadian Government having given permission because it was a NASA mission.

A second drone could only be flown from an aircraft carrier. No military activity was allowed in Antarctica because of the 1961 Antarctic treaty. The closest carrier group the, USS Abraham Lincoln based in the Southern Ocean, was still forty-six hours away at flank speed. The drone had been air lifted to the Lincoln and was now being assembled on board. Until the team at ISA had the *All Go* signal they turned their attention back to MATIS which was continuing to send information back.

Bruce entered the control room to find Kevin and Andy sat at the terminal responsible for receiving the packets of data from MATIS.

"Anything new?" Bruce asked them both.

"The anomaly is continuing to grow, but at an increasing rate," Kevin answered.

"How large an area is it covering?"

"We estimate forty-two thousand square meters," Andy answered.

"Two thousand square meters in three days," Bruce repeated as he sat at the opposite terminal.

In the accommodation block Jacob sat on his bed. He and Alice had taken some time for each other after the meeting with the President. It had become all too real for Jacob. Somehow telling the President had laid it all out in the open, and for Jacob that had meant it was no longer a theory that they were working on, now it was official. While Bruce and Jonathan had told the President that they didn't *believe* a solution could be found, Jacob knew there would be no way of stopping this if nature itself didn't. Alice had, as she promised she would, documented their findings and observations as well as the more mundane everyday life. Michael had insisted that even the small details should be documented for future generations. But with air travel now back to pre-event levels she needed to return home and to her family. Jacob didn't want her to leave, not only because he would miss her, but also because deep down, he was fearful that she would run the story once back in the U.K. and if she did it would put her and himself in danger. He watched her as she packed her luggage.

"You know they may not let you leave," Jacob said.

"I'm not so sure they can stop me."

"The President did tell us we were now bound by a Presidential order to keep this a secret."

"And I will. But Jacob I haven't seen my children or my family since last year and you know Skype isn't the same. I need to see them. Can't you understand that?"

"I guess, but what if they stop air traffic again in light of this anomaly. I won't see you again."

"They couldn't stop air traffic without telling people why, and if they did that we wouldn't need to keep it a secret, as the President has ordered. Look I promise it will be fine. I'll have a few months at home with my family; you know do the kids things, go to the park and the zoo.

Then I'll come back over and cover the rest of it," she said.

"And if we can't stop this from spreading? What will you do then?" Jacob asked.

"Jacob, you're one of the brightest men I have known, and you're working with the others, and you all have the President and NASA behind you. I'm sure this can be stopped."

He stretched out his hand and took hold of her fingers gently. "I'll miss you, you know," he said, softly.

Alice smiled. "And I'll miss you too. But I'll be back before you know it."

She picked up her luggage and left the room followed by Jacob. She entered the control room and said her goodbyes to Andy and Kevin. Michael and Bruce had left for a meeting with Jonathan, to update him on the information MATIS was sending back. "Okay guys, I'll see you in a month or two."

Kevin and Andy gave her hug and said the usual *we'll miss you and we'll keep in touch* stuff everybody says. Then they returned to their work. Jacob carried her luggage out to his car and placed it in the trunk. He pulled out of the Space Center and headed towards Washington and Dulles International. The Camry pulled up gently in the drop off zone and Alice unclipped her seatbelt. Jacob reached across and kissed her.

"Stay safe, and call me."

"You too, see you soon," Alice replied.

She climbed out of the car and having retrieved her luggage she waved and walked into the airport terminal. Jacob watched her until she was out of sight. Then he pulled away and returned to the Goddard Space Center.

Goddard Space Center

Bruce and Michael were in the trailer of the NASA Semi with the two pilots who were about to fly the drones. In the ISA control room, Jacob, Andy and Kevin were waiting for the data to be relayed to them. They knew that once they had all the information that the on-board instruments could collect it would be a race against time to have a brief prepared. The two pilots looked over to Michael.

"We're ready for take-off sir," the larger of the pilots announced.

"Okay then, here we go," Michael said, trying to hide his nerves. For the pilots, this was a routine training and evaluation flight. For Bruce and Michael this next hour would tell them the fate of our planet and all the life on it.

The first drone took off from Resolute Airport at 9:30 a.m. EST and headed towards the McGill Artic Research Station. With a flight time of three hours Bruce and Michael knew it would seem much more like three days. The second drone left the flight deck of the USS Abraham Lincoln at precisely the same time. The distance of the carrier to the coordinates in the Antarctic had been calculated carefully to ensure the flight time would be the same for both drones. For now, all Bruce and Michael and the team could do was wait. On the screens in front of the pilots the video feed showed the same bleak image: a white snow filled landscape. That was until at just under three hours after take-off.

The HD camera on the first drone showed an image of the large tent they had left behind, seconds later they could see the yellow snow cat and the research station. A few seconds later they saw the mangled wreck of the rescue chopper. Bruce's cell phone vibrated in his pocket. He looked down at the screen. It was a text from Jacob. "All data received," was all the message read.

As he placed the cell phone back in pocket the pilot of the drone over the research station began to sound concerned. "I'm losing power sir, the engine has died, I'm not sure why."

Bruce and Michael watched as he fought with the controls of the drone. But it was to no avail. The video feed showed the tent becoming larger as the drone headed for it, out of control. After only seconds the screen became blank and they knew that the drone had impacted with the tent. For Bruce and Michael, they also realized that it would mean the end to the data they were receiving from MATIS. As if to confirm this Bruce's cell vibrated once more. "Data from the drone stopped. Data from MATIS stopped." Bruce showed Michael the message from Jacob. Neither of them showed what they were feeling, they had to keep up the charade.

As the pilot of downed drone sat back clearly frustrated, the second pilot announced that he had arrived at the coordinates over the Antarctic.

"I've arrived sir, what do you want me to do now?"

"Just circle for now," Bruce said.

"I'll try sir, but I'm getting unusually heavy buffeting for this area sir. I'm not sure how long I'll be able to keep lift under the wings sir."

Bruce looked at Michael. This wasn't a good sign. This high-altitude turbulence might be sign of the anomaly drawing air from the atmosphere.

"I'm gaining altitude sir. I'm going to lose the drone if I can't correct this," the pilot said.

"Why are you gaining altitude?" Michael asked.

"I don't know sir, something is pulling me up."

As he spoke the video screen showed nothing more than a blurry spinning image of blue and white. They could clearly see that the drone was caught in some sort of ferocious turbulence. After a few seconds, the image began to steady, and as a view of space came into focus the screen became blank and all readings on the pilot's console reset back to zero.

"I don't understand this sir; the drone has gone. But I don't know where, it didn't crash."

"What was your last altitude reading?" Bruce asked.

The pilot brought up the drone's flight log. "One hundred Kilometers sir, sixty-two miles," he answered.

Bruce turned to Michael, "The Kaman Line."

As he spoke his cell phone vibrated, he looked at the incoming message from Jacob. "All data received from the second drone." Bruce pushed the phone back into his pocket. Then he turned to the pilots. "What happened to these drones today? You don't tell anyone," he said.

"We lost two drones sir, we have to file a report why they crashed," the first pilot said.

"No, I'll do that, you have special dispensation on this one. Do you understand?" Bruce asked.

"Yes sir."

Bruce and Michael left the trailer and headed back to the ISA control room. Inside Jacob, Andy and Kevin were sat waiting for them.

"What did we get from the drones?" Bruce asked them.

"The second drone was flying steady at fifteen thousand feet, but once it entered the coordinates its altitude increased at a hell of a rate, and then the data stream stopped. It's as if it was pulled up and out of the atmosphere," Jacob said.

"But we did get what we needed?" Michael asked.

"Yes, we did." Andy answered him.

"Okay, you and Kevin collate it all today, I'll call Jonathan and schedule a meeting tomorrow with the President," Bruce said to Andy.

"Okay, will do boss."

Chapter 12
The Oval Office: The White House, Washington DC

February 14th, 2023. 11:00 a.m.

Ten days had passed since the *Resolute incident* as it had come to be known and four days had passed since Bruce had told the President that the world was likely to suffer the same fate as Mars, becoming a barren and lifeless rock floating through space around a sun that once gave life, but had now taken it away. But he had not finished giving the President the bad news. After the drone flights and putting their data with the data that MATIS had collected, they had now finished their equations. They had the figure that would determine how long mankind would have left if no way could be found to seal the rift in the earth's atmosphere. Bruce, Michael and Jacob would now have the task of telling the President, and this wasn't a conversation they were looking forward to. In what seemed like a short period of time Bruce had found himself going from the head of the first manned mission to Mars, to being the herald of the apocalypse.

Bruce sat in the Oval Office with Michael and Jacob. As before, four dark suited secret service men stood silently in the background. They arrived an hour before the planned meeting and briefed Jonathan on what they'd learnt from the drones and from MATIS before it was destroyed. And like Bruce, Jonathan was pensive, he realized now in detail what their summation was, and like Bruce it had shook him to his core.

The door that led to the President's private office opened and President Young entered, accompanied as always by his private aid and General Scott. As before Bruce, Michael, Jacob and Jonathan stood.

"Hello Bruce. What have you got to tell me?" the President asked as he sat behind his desk.

"Hello Mr President. I'll make it short as I'm sure you'll have enough to fill your day once I tell you what we have calculated."

"Thank you. I would appreciate it if you would. Firstly, I am told you lost both drones and the equipment that was monitoring the research station."

"Do we know why the drones crashed?" General Scott asked.

"Only one crashed General, the drone over the research station at Resolute crashed for the same reason the helicopter went down, loss of power," Michael said.

"And the second drone?" asked the General.

"Its systems went down when it reached the Kaman Line," Jacob answered.

"What is that?" President Young asked.

"The Kaman Line is sixty-two miles above the earth, and is generally accepted as the end of our atmosphere, and the start of space," Jacob answered.

"I don't understand, why would the drone be at that altitude?" General Scott asked.

"The rift that is responsible for pulling the atmosphere out into space pulled the drone up, and displaced it in outer space sir," Jacob said.

"If the drone is in space, why can't we use its instruments?" General Scott asked.

"No General, I'm afraid the forces involved would have torn the drone apart. By now it will just be fragments," Jonathan said.

"Now tell me what I need to know Bruce. What conclusions have you come to, based on the information that you received?" President Young answered.

"Mr President. We have cut the overall time scale into three time events; one is the time scale for North America, two is the time it will take the anomaly to reach the equator, and the last is the time it will take to fully engulf the earth sir, the complete death of every living thing on this planet, with the exception of some forms of bacteria."

"What do mean, bacteria, Bruce?" President Young asked.

"It is thought, Mr President that life on earth started with space bacteria that was introduced by asteroids as they impacted the earth. It is highly probable, even completely correct to say that we believe some of that bacterium is still alive on earth sir. And there are parts of the deep ocean where there is no oxygen and yet there is bacterial life."

"So, *we* all die. A species that can and has achieved all that we have, but a single cell, hell not even that, just some microscopic bacteria, might beat us?" President Young asked.

Bruce didn't know how to respond. As a scientist, he'd been a firm atheist for most of his life, but now that firm rock to which he'd anchored himself was shaken to its core, the thought of the President's questions, and the consequences for all of mankind should it be true, started to haunt him.

Recognizing that his last statement and question had unnerved an unprepared Bruce, the President changed the subject, and brought the conversation back to why Bruce had called. It was time now to hear the predictions that would determine the end of us as individuals, and as a species.

"Ok Bruce, give me the time scales. I've put you on speaker with Vice President Wilson. I filled him in on the situation after our last meeting, but I want him to hear this as I do," President Young said.

"Okay Mr President. Here is the information. Given the earth measures approximately five hundred million square meters, and the anomaly is expanding at a rate of..."

"Bruce, just give me numbers. I do not need the calculation. All I am interested in, all I need is the result, just give me the date," the President interrupted.

"Sorry Mr President. Here is where we are. After using the drones and the robot, the anomaly hasn't stopped increasing. The vacuum is now acting like an open window on an aircraft at altitude. What I mean to say sir is that the earth's atmosphere is now leaking out into space through the vacuum, as I feared when we first met a few days ago, our atmosphere will eventually dissipate. To put it literally Mr President, our planet is going to suffocate. As for the time scales, we expect that the U.S. will be unable to support life by late September this year, the northern hemisphere around the end of

January next year, and the planet by early July next year. That is based on the current estimate, which is subject to changes."

The room became silent. It was the same silence that Bruce and his team had experienced in the office when they'd first seen the predictions the super computer at the Goddard Space Center had produced.

President Young now felt a stirring of emotions that were a mix of dread, anger and defeat in the knowledge that no one else on earth, apart those present in this room, and the Vice President, knew what fate awaited our planet.

"Are you telling me that this is it Bruce, that we have less than a year?" President Young asked.

"It's our best guess sir. If the anomaly stops growing, if the rift in the atmosphere closes then maybe, just maybe only the most northerly parts of our hemisphere would be affected until the planet could stabilize and regenerate. But given what we know and the information we have, I'm sorry sir, I just don't see it happening."

"What about you Jonathan, do you agree?" President Young asked.

"Yes, sir I do. I concur completely."

President Young clasped his hands together and brought his closed fists down on the desk. "God dam it," he shouted.

Bruce looked among his team. He hadn't seen the President act this way before, but given what he had just been told, how else could he react?

"Can we close the rift?" General Scott asked.

"How would you do that?" Jonathan asked.

"A nuclear detonation, perhaps the blast would force it closed?" General Scott answered.

"No, it would accelerate it, and besides even our largest weapons are insignificant to the forces we're dealing with," Michael said.

"To confirm gentlemen, you believe there is nothing further we can do to halt or even delay this?" President Young asked.

"I'm sorry sir; we just don't have the technology," Jonathan answered.

"And those time scales you have given me, that's your best guess?" President Young asked.

"At the current rate the planet uses the oxygen. Yes, sir," Bruce answered.

"At the rate which we use oxygen?" President Young asked.

"Yes sir. If you take all the internal combustion engines in the world for instance, each of those engines use oxygen to complete the combustion cycle, any power stations which burn to produce steam, which turn the turbines to produce the electricity, the burning process, whether it be coal, oil or wood, the resulting fire consumes oxygen, but by far the largest use would be by us sir, human beings, every one of us; the young, the old, even the dying sir, and all of the animal life too."

"The dying, Bruce?" The President pushed on that example.

"People in hospices or on life support systems sir, pets, livestock the list is endless."

"Okay. Thank you, Bruce. You have been of great service to your country. You all have, and I know how difficult this was especially with some of you having families. Knowing almost to the hour when you will perish is one of mankind's greatest paradoxes. Should you know when you are going to die, would you want to know? Up until last week I had always fought with that. I was never sure if I would or not, but now that information is here, written by my own hand, I am now sure I didn't want to know. I want you to continue to work with Jonathan and keep me informed of any changes in the rift or the anomaly, anything that would indicate it slowing down or gaining in speed, or of course closing."

"We will continue as long as we can Mr President. But with the drones gone and the robot that we stationed at Resolute destroyed, we no longer have any direct measuring capability. We are currently redirecting two military spy satellites; one will be stationed as close to the rift as is possible, the other will be above Resolute. The instrumentation on board isn't sufficient for what we need sir, but it's the best we can do, we don't have time to develop, build and launch a new satellite," Bruce assured him.

Outside the Oval Office Bruce shook Jonathan's hand "I'll be in touch Jonathan, once we have the satellites hooked in."

"Do you think it will slow or stop Bruce?" Jonathan asked.

Bruce let go of his hand shook his head. "No, I don't," he whispered.

Back at the Goddard Flight Center Bruce had one more task that he had to complete and he was dreading it as much as he had the last. Now they had the time scales and the President had been briefed, Bruce needed call the crew of SOL 1 and bring them up to date with what was about to happen.

Mission control had kept in close contact with the crew, and their families too had been updating them on the events in their home countries and from around the world. But, no one knew the end game outside ISA and the President.

Bruce sat in front of a large monitor as ready as he would ever be to make this call. It was not normal for the head of a mission to call un-expectantly during the mission. He knew that as soon as his I.D showed as the caller, the team would know that something was not right. Sighing he hit the mouse button and watched as the icon disappeared and was replaced by the large viewing screen, which would show an image of them once connected along with a much smaller screen in the top left corner, which showed Bruce an image of himself. The large blue view-screen started to pixelate into an image of Commander Jake Iverson, whom he had last seen in the final hours before take-off.

"Commander Iverson hello, can you see and hear me ok?"

"That is positive Mr McCaughey."

With the comms check completed Bruce began what he had to do.

"Commander Iverson, where are the rest of the team? What I have to say involves all of you. They need to join you."

"I'll bring them in sir."

Bruce watched as the crew gathered around their Commander.

"We're all here and ready sir," Commander Iverson said.

Bruce began. "You remember last year the earth was hit by a massive and previously un-registered CME, and that along with many satellites the ISS and her crew were lost. What we didn't tell you back then, because we did not know, was that the magnetosphere which had already been weakened by the propulsion system on SOL 1, had in fact been damaged or ripped. The damage to the magnetosphere happened above the South Pole, Antarctica where your main engines fired. We now know that was where the storm hit the hardest because of the tilt of the earth along its orbit of the sun. The effects of this are that a vacuum has formed on the surface of the earth, a funnel of space if you can imagine, which came through our atmosphere and reached down to the surface. It killed the three members of the team that ran a research station, and a helicopter pilot who had been dispatched to rescue them after they'd failed to communicate. Do you understand so far?"

Bruce took a breath. He turned his face away from the camera for a second so he could once again compose himself. He knew he had eighteen seconds before that message would reach them, and then another eighteen before he would get their reply. Even though this was old news to Bruce, who with his team had first discovered it and then informed the President, it still seemed to be getting more difficult each time he had to inform someone of it. Still he'd wondered to himself; should telling someone that you know they are going to die and when be easy? Should walking around with this knowledge and not being able to explode it in to the public domain be easy?

He'd always come to the same conclusion; No, it shouldn't. It should be the hardest thing any man with any compassion is expected to do. He turned back to the monitor, a single tear had left a mark on his face from where he had hastily wiped it away before continuing.

The answer came back, "Yes sir we understand, please carry on."

"The vacuum I've just described is not stationary. It is continuing to expand. The earth's atmosphere is being sucked out of the vacuum and into space and there is nothing we can do to stop it or close it. We anticipate that the United States will be sterile and lifeless by late September this year. The northern hemisphere will be lifeless sometime in January next year, and all life on earth will cease in the early days of July, next year."

Bruce tried hard to keep his resolve for the faces that now looked at him with expressions of disbelief. He was now becoming weary, He watched their expressions change from disbelief to the same expression he had seen on everyone else he'd given this news to: disbelief then the realization that they, their families, friends and loved ones were going to die soon and shortly after this all life on earth would end.

Bruce continued. "Commander Iverson, even if you leave today, which we know you cannot because of your prep time, you will not arrive back in earth's orbit until August. There is no way you can get back here before then. And, as I've stated the U.S. will be a void a few weeks later. For this reason, we are currently making arrangements to have your families flown to Australia. Flight command are working on new orbit and landing co-ordinates that will see you land in the Australian Western

Territories in the Badjaling Nature Reserve just east of Perth. At least there you will have around eleven months before Australia is consumed."

Bruce became silent again allowing the stunned crew to respond.

"Sir, if we understand you correctly, you have just told us that the world is going to end in a little over seventeen months? And that you are taking us to Australia? Which family members are you taking, who gets to decide sir?"

Bruce now felt shocked and knocked back. They had all been knocked physically sick when they'd come to the conclusions which he'd now presented to the President and the Martialis crew. He knew their reaction would be more measured than the President's, because these people were carefully selected for their ability to remain calm in any emergency during their missions. They had what the average person would call, *nerves of steel*. The coolness of any super hero and of course, for this mission because of the unprecedented nature of it, they all had to be single. Still, Bruce had expected that they would have reacted more than they had. Hell! They should now be screaming down the line at him or swearing, something, anything. He continued to deliver the facts.

"It is affirmative commander; this is not a drill or exercise. This is a real event, and it is happening. As for Australia, those details will be up to you. Whoever you choose, these family members must adhere to keeping this a secret. Any leak to the public will cause anarchy in the literal sense. We will move them, and it will be done in secret to avoid any safety concerns for them. Here's the thing Jake, I need you and your crew to let me know who it is you want to move to Perth. Because of logistics you must choose no more than four people each. I will contact you in twenty-four hours to get your decisions. In the meantime, I need you all to come to terms with what you have just been told. Until tomorrow, Commander."

Once Bruce saw the confirmation that his last message had been transmitted, he clicked the icon that closed the interplanetary communications. Jake's somber expression was replaced by the background wallpaper of the PC. Bruce sighed as he pushed the mouse away from his hand. His role now in the remaining months that the earth had left consisted of counting down to the inevitable. Bruce headed home, drained and defeated.

SOL 1: habitat control hub.
225 million km from earth.

The crew of SOL 1 sat in silence as they each processed the information they'd been given.

Sergey broke the delicate silence. "What the hell do we do now?"

"There isn't a great deal we can other than what we've been asked to do," Jake answered.

"That's it, it's just the end?" Joe said.

"We should leave immediately; get back as quickly as we can," Sergey said.

"You know we cannot do that, we'd have to prep and wait for the main propulsion drive to orbit back around, and for the Earth and Mars to re-align," Jake replied.

"And besides, you heard the message, America and most of Europe will be a wasteland shortly after we achieve earth orbit, even if we could leave now," Mary said.

"But what about our families? Are you saying we should just sit here knowing how they're going to die?" Sergey asked.

"What would you do to save them? We are three months from home, and if we did get back and by some miracle we did manage we beat the vacuum before it moved through the northern hemisphere how would you save them?" Joseph asked.

"I don't know, fly them out."

"By then any and all transport of that kind will be compromised, air traffic will likely be grounded and the road and rail network will have ground to a halt under the pressure of the number of people trying to flee," Jake said.

"But it's unfair to ask which of our family members should be saved," Sergey said.

"Yes, it is, but ultimately, they won't be saved, will they? At least we get to be with someone we love when the time comes," Joe said.

The room became silent again as each of them now understood they had only one choice. They had to choose who would have the additional time with them in Australia, and who would perish as the anomaly crept over the planet killing everything in its path.

Sergey checked his watch, which was set to Greenwich Mean Time, the time zone NASA used with astronauts traveling in space. "It is twenty-three hundred hours. It is time for me to decide who in my family I want with me when the end comes, so I will bid you a good-night."

Jake smiled at Sergey and watched as he left. Chun followed with a nod as he too left for his quarters.

"I'm going to bed too, goodnight," Mary said.

"Is this happening Jake? How can it be that the world is ending in our life time?" Joe asked.

"Honestly? I think it's just bad luck," Jake replied, devoid of any scientific or philosophical answers.

"Bad luck?"

"Yeah! Think about it. First SOL 1 causes an effect that no one expected. Second, before the magnetosphere can fully recover, the earth is hit by a massive solar storm unlike any that happened before. Imagine Joe, right the way back, right back to when apes first started to walk upright, and then all of the generations through time that led directly to us, all the chance meetings that lead to marriage and child birth throughout our family trees, even the fact that out of the millions of sperm our fathers released, that it was us that came to be, imagine if your parents had not had sex right at that specific time. None of us on board this ship, on this mission, would be here. If that rule applied to the person that designed the propulsion system, then this whole eventuality that has taken us to this point would not be. But here's the thing Joe, is it all just chance? Surely, even the most passionate atheist could not deny the beauty of those circumstances?"

Joe sighed and lifted his head from his hands and looked through the port window into the Martian night's sky, and then he looked back to Jake.

"And you know the worst thing Jake?"

Jake shook his head slowly.

"When seven billion people do die on earth, all of them crying out with an ear-piercing scream as the planet dies, out here, out in the vast cosmos, we will pass silently and unknown. All that will be left of mankind's greatest achievements will be a few robots and discarded tech on long distant planets and moons. There will be nothing to carry on our species legacy. And what saddens me is that our greatest accomplishment of all, the written word and languages of all of earth's cultures, will be lost forever. It will ultimately have been for nothing," Joe said.

"Not necessarily."

"What do you mean?"

"Voyager one, launched September 1977, has now passed out of our solar system, along with Voyager two, though in the opposite direction. Both are now in deep space, and still sending data back. Their on-board systems are still functional. But more importantly, it is what they carry with them. They took with them the essence of mankind; music, information about earth, all of our cultures, our fears and beliefs, and our art as well as our language. The most widely used language, English. And on Voyager two our DNA. As long as those two small ships continue through the endlessness of the cosmos, mankind will still be among the stars. One day, when they are picked up by an alien race, we will live on with them. But after we go, they truly will be, alone in the universe."

"I'm going to turn in now. Seems I have some thinking to do," Joe said.

As Joe left and walked from the main hub into the small corridor that lead to the accommodation pods, Mary caught his attention and he followed her in the kitchen. They had become attracted to each other during the early days of the mission, but had not acted on it because they knew that it was strictly against mission protocols to be involved with a crew member. Feelings like these would put the mission and other crew members lives in danger for a whole raft of reasons. But once they'd arrived on

Mars they had started a secret relationship, hiding it was the best thing to do, it could cause resentment among the other crew members and it would put Jake in an impossible position should an emergency strike and he had to make a call that put either of them in jeopardy. But they'd had their chances in the fourteen months they'd been on the surface.

"Joe, I have had a thought we should discuss."

"What is it?"

"I think we should stay here when the others leave for home."

"But what about our families?"

"Do you want to watch them die in that way, do you want to die like that?"

Joe thought for a moment. How could anyone watch the people they love die such a horrible death? "No of course I don't," he answered.

"There's something else."

"What is it?"

Mary took hold of Joe's hand and pulled him toward her placing it on her stomach. "I'm two months pregnant, it happened when we were out by the Mawrth Vallis with the robot. Remember? We spent the night in the roamer? So, you see going back would mean killing our child."

Joe leant on the kitchen counter. Then checking that the coast was clear, he put his arms around her and kissed her gently. "Then you're right, we have to stay here." He said.

Mary kissed him back.

"I'm not going to tell anyone. They will have begun their journey home before I start to show. And besides, I doubt they'll notice in the activity to get away."

"I think that's best," he agreed.

Jake left the main hub and was soon in his own living pod, which consisted of a small room with basic but essential equipment, including a high definition screen linked to the main frame that could stream almost every album and movie ever produced. They also had private screens allowing them to talk to their friends and family, and each pod was decorated according to their own personal tastes.

This was the one place in the whole complex that didn't look like a typical NASA designed all white space prison. Jake climbed into the semi enclosed compartment that formed the comfortable bed. Looking up directly above him he touched a button on the control pad. An external blast screen slid back revealing a window, allowing Jake to stare at what was to him a night sky on Mars. He pushed another button and music started to play. Dimming his lights, he fell asleep staring into the Martian sky, while in the background the song, *Narrow Daylight*, played softly.

Another day started on Mars. Like every other morning, before they had breakfast, they checked the essential systems. Then, they would normally go about their assigned duties to ensure that this small habitat can sustain them on this hostile and barren planet. But that morning, after checks, the normal routine ended. The crew made their way back to the main control room and waited for the call that would come from Bruce. Together, they would tell him which family members they each wanted relocating to Australia. Each of them sat around the large screen waiting for the incoming call. After a short time, the screen changed from the screensaver, which consisted of the Martialis mission logo, to a window which said *Incoming Transmission.*

"Good morning SOL 1. I hope this finds you as well as can be expected given the circumstances."

"Good Morning Sir. I guess we are. None of us have had much sleep, deciding which family members to save isn't something that is conducive to a good night's sleep," Jake said.

Jake turned to each of them and asked them to hand him their lists detailing the four family members that will be transported to Australia. Then he turned back to the screen and read out the lists.

"Okay Bruce, here are the details you will need. Firstly, myself." Jake started to read the list of names that for a short while at least would be saved from the approaching anomaly. "Hope that is clear Bruce?"

As Jake handed back the pieces of paper he made sure not to crumple them, or risk showing any disrespect to the names on them. As far his own list, he looked at it one last time and then crumpled it and put it into the waste bin. He turned back to the monitor and counted down the remaining seconds for Bruce to confirm their transmission, but as slow as it was watching the last few seconds' tick down, they did, and the screen eventually showed Bruce's image as it had done yesterday.

"Hi Jake, yes I can confirm we have got your list and have successfully taken the names. I can also confirm that flight control sent the data package which they tell me SOL 1's systems have successfully uploaded and over-ridden the original flight programme. SOL 1 will now take you to the new destination east of Perth, Australia. You have a mission go for fourteen-thirty hours your time on March 26th. Because of the secretive nature of this you will be contacted only at the half-way point of your journey home. We must maintain radio silence until you are contacted, and when you are it will not be by a U.S. based station. It will be by a selective flight operations crew. To that end Jake, this will be the last time we will speak. I wish you Gods speed and a safe journey back to earth. Good luck Jake."

"You too Bruce, good luck to all on earth."

Jake then turned to his crew who sat silently, still holding their own pieces of paper with the names of the family members they'd chosen to live a little longer. Each of them wished with every fiber of their being that they hadn't had too.

"Okay, you all heard what Bruce said. I suggest you secure the base, shut down all experiments, and prep for departure. Joe, I want you to check the data package and make sure the systems, and auto pilot are set correctly for Australia. Okay people; we have things to complete. Let's get to them."

February 21st, 2023: 7:44 p.m. GMT.

"Jake, Jake. Can Mary and I have five minutes?" Joe called after Jake as he headed through the hydroponics bay, which had kept them supplied with water, food and fresh oxygen, and was a secondary system to the main air filtration system. Hydroponics took the largest of the out reaching arms that led from the lander section of SOL 1. Jake stopped and spun around to see Mary and Joe catching up to him. From their expressions Jake, could tell that this was a conversation that wouldn't wait.

"Yes of course, what is it?"

"It's about returning home early," Joe told him.

"Okay what about it?"

"We have decided that we don't want to go back to earth. We'd like to stay here on Mars and keep this base running."

Jake, confused by Joe's request, asked for confirmation of what he'd just been told. "You want to do what?"

"We want to stay here on this station; we're not going back to earth," Mary said.

"Why? Surely you can't expect to live a full life here. Don't you want to be with your family? What about the four names you both gave to NASA?" Jake asked.

"Well it is like this Jake; we do not want to go back to earth to die with our families. We would rather live here and take our chances," Mary said.

"But I don't think that I can sanction this. Our orders are quite clear."

"There will be no orders after you get back to earth, you know that," Joe said.

"You know everybody on board is vital to the safety of the ship, being two crew down would endanger all of our safety," Jake said.

"You know you can make it without us. Mary is a geologist, you know she's not critical to the flight."

"But you're the flight engineer, you are," Jake replied.

"I'm your second, you know the systems as well as me, and the flight path is already laid in. You don't need us."

Mary turned to Joe, and took his hand. "I should tell him."

"No, we agreed that wouldn't be a good idea."

"Tell me what?" Jake asked.

"There's something you should know before you say anything else," Mary said.

She looked at Joe and then back to Jake. "I'm expecting our child."

Jake felt betrayed, let down by his second in command. "How long?" he asked.

"Since we landed, we kept it hidden." Joe said.

Jake sighed and shrugged. What else could he do, he couldn't condemn their unborn child to a certain death, and he knew Joe was right. They could make the trip without him.

"I'll tell them when they contact us at the half-way point. I see no reason to do it before we leave," Jake said.

"Thank you," Mary said.

Jake didn't respond, he simply nodded, accepting, and even agreeing with their decision. He turned and headed back toward the main hub and to Sergey to get an update on the propulsion system.

March 20th, 2023. 2:30 p.m. GMT.

"Five, four, three, two, one. We have a clean and successful take off. Next stop Australia. To Joe and Mary, good luck," Jake said over the comms.

"Thank you. Please tell our families, why we stayed, and that we love them," Joe said.

Outside of the habitat and dressed in their planetary suits, designed for the conditions on Mars, Joe and Mary watched until SOL 1 had vanished from view. To them the ship was a brilliant white light racing back out into deep space and away from them. While outside, they took the time to check the structure of what would now be their permanent home. With no way to leave Mars, they had become the first humans to permanently occupy another planet. This structure, that was no larger than perhaps what would be considered a modest home back on earth, was now their own private Eden. With all of the checks completed they entered through the air lock, sealing them inside and away from the hostile world outside. They removed their suits and without saying anything to each other they smiled, held hands and made their way through the hub and toward the living quarters.

Chapter 13

April 18th, 2023. 9:13 a.m. EST.

Jacob entered the ISA control room and walked to the coffee machine. He had that depressed feeling that today would be the same as the rest of them had become. He felt like a hamster on a wheel, the work they were doing was vital but it would also prove to be ultimately futile, because the outcome now was certain. The two satellites they had positioned had confirmed their worst fears. The anomaly was continuing its path of devastation across the northern hemispheres and the rift was holding steady and showing no signs of closing. He picked up the coffee and took it over to where Andy and Kevin were sat.

"Hi," Jacob said as he sat at his desk.

"Have you seen this?" Kevin asked Jacob.

"How the hell would I know what *this* is?" Jacob said, taking a sip of coffee.

"I think you should."

Jacob put his coffee down and moved across to Kevin's desk. "What am I looking at?" he asked.

"Andy and I were looking into the details of SOL 1's engines, you know, the problems Steve said they could cause."

"Why were you doing that? Don't you think we have enough to do?" Jacob asked.

"The data was running in the background, so we started poking around, looking to see if we were able to find the original reports. We thought they may help find a way of closing the rift."

"What is it you've found?"

"This!" Kevin said as he pointed to the screen.

Jacob moved to where he could clearly see what was on the large flat screen. As he read it his stomach turned over and he felt a wave of heat rise through him. He recognized it. It was the same realization some people describe at the point when they have been in real mortal danger, and Jacob had felt it when the FBI had pulled Alice and him over. The report, by General Scott, detailed the real reasons why the Martialis mission was pushed through and why the testing of the engines had been altered to show none of the complications detailed by Steve David. He had hoped that when Steve had visited him after he was sacked his rant about establishing nuclear weapons on Mars had just been a fantasy. Perhaps for that reason more than any other Jacob had dismissed it and not told anyone what Steve had said. But now he could see that he was telling him the truth, and this kind of information was dangerous.

He turned to Kevin and Andy. "Have you shown this to anyone else?"

"No, just you," Andy answered.

"Thank Christ, don't! Save the file to a private hidden folder, in case we need it sometime later. In the meantime, pretend like you don't know a fucking thing. Information like this could get you killed."

He left the control room and headed outside. He sat in his car and pulled out his cell phone. Pressing Alice's speed dial number, he placed his phone down onto the dashboard and set it on loud speaker. After a few rings, she answered.

"Hi, Jacob?" It was Alice, thank God, she had finally answered.

"Shush Alice, listen to me carefully."

"Okay secret agent man, I'm listening," Alice replied.

Alice still wasn't taking Jacob seriously and he was running out of patience.

"Where are you?" he asked.

"I'm packing my luggage to come back over to the States."

"When is your flight?"

"I should be landing at Dulles tomorrow morning, around nine a.m. local time."

"Don't say the place, just confirm if you remember where we met the last time you came in."

"I do." She replied.

"Don't tell anyone where you're going."

"Jacob, what's going on? The last time you were like this the FBI pulled us over."

"I'll explain tomorrow, but listen, when you land go to the place and stay there. I will be there to meet you. And Alice."

"Yes?" she said.

"Do not deviate from my directions."

Before Alice had a chance to confirm, Jacob hung up.

April 19th, 2023. 9:28 a.m. EST. Dulles International Airport, Washington DC. Main Entrance.

Jacob rushed through the automatic doors scouting among the many faces for the one he knew so well. As the blurred sea of faces rushed by him, all in a hurry, each of them doing what at that time was so important, he felt a panic rise inside him

"Boo!" Alice shouted excitedly as she grabbed him around his waist from behind.

Jacob jumped. He was on edge, and being grabbed in an international airport didn't make him any less so.

"Jesus, you scared me," Jacob said. But Alice's smile calmed him.

"What's with the cloak and dagger routine Jacob? You sounded peculiar," Alice asked.

"I'll explain when we're back at my place," he said turning and heading for the exit.

Jacob guided Alice to his car. They set off on the short drive back to the apartment he'd rented while he'd been attached to the small task force with Bruce and the others. He entered along with Alice and looked around one last time, then pulled the curtains across, and sat holding out his arm, he invited her to sit in the chair opposite. The apartment was of a decent size, with the kitchen part of the main living area. It was large enough to break up the open plan layout with a large dining table and couch. In the living area was the usual A/C unit and flat screen TV that hung on the wall with an unbranded Blu-ray player under it. An open fireplace on the opposite wall provided the room with a warm focal point on a winter's day. Down a small corridor were two bedrooms and a bathroom. Alice sat opposite Jacob on a large soft couch and placed her laptop on the coffee table between them, ready for her to report anything Jacob was about to say.

"Okay, I'm here so what's the big mystery?" she asked.

Jacob reached into his satchel that was next to his chair and pulled out a large neat pile of paper. He placed it down next to Alice's laptop and pushed it toward her.

"This is a document that Kevin came across while he was searching Steve David's files. He was looking for the original test reports of the engines to see if that data would help produce some sort of theory on how to close the rift." He took a breath. "This paperwork details why the Martialis Mission was rushed through the pipeline, and why the engine tests were falsified and changed. Steve David was correct, and they knew it, Bruce and Jonathan, the fucking lot of them knew it, and they ignored it," Jacob said.

"But why would they do that?"

"For the real reason, they were in a hurry to get to Mars."

"And what's that?" Alice asked.

"The U.S. wanted to be the first to build a strategic tactical weapons platform. A launch from Mars using the same propulsion system deployed in SOL 1 would leave us completely dominant. No country would dare show hostility towards the U.S. or her allies, and believe me there would be a lot of countries wanting to be our allies. We could charge any price we wanted to join our club; oil, gas any resource on this planet, or any other would be ours," Jacob explained.

Alice sat back in the couch. "If I've got this straight, they understood the propulsion system could have an effect on our planet but they pushed ahead anyway and in despite of Steve David's warnings so they could plant weapons on Mars and hold the world to ransom?"

"Yes. I mean they didn't know about the CME because RHESSI had failed, but essentially if the engines had been tested properly and the mission had followed the safe guards, then the CME wouldn't have caused the rift over Antarctica."

"Who knows about this?" Alice asked.

"Myself, Kevin, Andy and now you, as well as those who took the decisions, Bruce and a few others."

"Do you think President Young knows?" Alice asked.

"I can't see how he wouldn't be."

Jacob dropped his head down and let out a sigh. He realized now that he had told her, he had opened Pandora's Box, and like the tale itself, there was no going back.

Alice picked up the paper and started to read it. As she did the usual thoughts rushed through her mind, raising the questions without answers. The planet was going to die. It was to suffocate in the vacuum of space, and while she'd managed to come to terms with that as an accident, as an oversight because of the use of a previously unused propulsion system, and an unprecedented solar storm. The thought that all life would end because the government would gain control of all of earth's natural resources by holding all other countries to ransom became too much for her. Alice emptied the contents of her stomach over her laptop and Jacob's table. Then, she passed out and slumped forward, and off the couch.

April 19th, 2023. 11:38 a.m. EST.

In Greenbelt, Michael had just met with Bruce. Kevin had told Michael of what he'd found and his plans to go live on a blog with the information. Michael had pleaded with him not to do it, but when he'd received a text from Kevin yesterday with a link to the URL, Michael knew he would be in serious trouble. Immediately, he'd called Bruce, the one man he believed he could trust, and asked him to meet the next day at Ruby Tuesday's, an American diner, not too far from the Goddard Space Center.

Though Michael had been hesitant to talk to Bruce over his cell phone about why he wanted to meet him, Bruce was reluctant to meet up until he knew what the reason was.

Michael pulled his Range Rover in the parking lot stopping opposite Greenbelt road. He locked it and walked into the diner where he found Bruce waiting for him. He sat next to him in one of those typical diner booths.

"Are you sure what Kevin has seen?" Bruce asked.

"I am, he showed me the reports Bruce."

"Can you just tell me one more time what he showed you?"

Michael explained in great detail what Kevin had shown him. "What should we do? Should we go to Jonathan or even the President? We could get into a shit load of trouble even knowing this," Michael said.

Bruce reassured him. "Leave it with me, do nothing for now, I'll speak with Jonathan, test the mood and then we'll decide. Is Kevin at home now?"

"Yes, I told him and Andy to wait at home until I'd spoken with you."

Bruce smiled. "Okay, leave it at that. And thanks for coming to me with this."

"Ok, I'm just a little nervous you know, you hear things like this and what happens. I gotta tell you I'm looking over shoulder a bit."

"It'll be fine," Bruce assured him.

Michael stood and went to the toilet. Once he'd left the booth Bruce picked up his cell and called Jonathan. "Did you get all of that?"

"I did. General Scott is here with me. We'll send agents to pick up Kevin and Andy." Jonathan said.

"And Michael?" Bruce asked.

"It's taken care of" General Scott answered.

Bruce hung up as Michael appeared from the toilet entrance. As he passed Bruce he nodded, "I'll see you back at ISA later," he said.

"You will," Bruce replied.

Michael left the diner sure he'd done the right thing. With Bruce in the loop, and his assurance he would talk to Jonathan he felt the responsibility that he'd reluctantly taken on had been passed up the command chain. He unlocked his Range Rover and climbed in. Switching on the ignition he started the engine.

By the time Michael's body registered the explosion from under the SUV, he was already engulfed in the resulting fire ball. And though he had just a Nano-second to process the thoughts of a scream, he didn't have the time to form it. As the blast wave pushed him through the already detached driver's door Michael Forbes was dead.

Alice woke a while later, on Jacob's bed. She sat up as Jacob entered with a glass of water and noticed that she is wearing one of his t-shirts. Still a little foggy headed, she took the water off him and sipped a little.

"I see you changed my top, any excuse Jacob. Where's my laptop?" Alice asked.

"In the bin, along with your lovely smelly cotton blouse."

"The bin? Everything is on my laptop! My whole bloody life!"

"Sorry. The urm, watery bits of your vomit shorted out the mainboard. I did pull the hard drive out before I threw it away."

"Thank God. Will you be able to access it, or at least the folders?"

"I have. I put it in a caddy and plugged it into mine, but listen. I have to get to Kevin. While you were sleeping, I received a message from him. He's put the information on line in a blog. I don't think he knows how much trouble he's in by doing that, I've tried to get back on it, but the URL isn't connecting to anything."

"Give me two minutes and I'll come with you. I want to talk him, and then I have to decide what to do with what you've told me," Alice replied.

"Decide? What do you mean? I hadn't got the bit I wanted to tell you before you blew chunks and blacked out."

"What do you mean? What else is there?" she asked.

"I can get you to Australia with me; they're taking the team so we can track it. But you weren't on the list. I've e-mailed you the documents you will need."

Alice cut Jacob off before he explained.

"Australia! Jacob, I have children. I can't just abandon them; I can't leave them to, to suffer."

Alice said sadly, but in a firm non-negotiable manner, but she couldn't finish the sentence. She couldn't bring herself to say any sentence that had the words children, and die.

"I'll come with you to see Kevin and then I'll catch a flight home. I should get back now to the protection of the U.K. for the story. The truth has to be told Jacob. Surely you see that, don't you?" she finished.

Jacob looked at her despondently. He had hoped she would follow him to Australia. He had never thought for a single second that she wouldn't be with him when the world ended. The thought that he would be with Alice at the end had kept him going. It was the one single thing that had given him the strength he needed. In the same way some people found comfort in the belief that they would ascend to heaven and be with their loved ones, Jacob had found the same strength in Alice's arms. But now that had been taken away from him as well, and he felt fragile and betrayed.

"You don't need to Alice, just go home. You have your story there's no reason for you to stay now."

"No. I'll still come with you Jacob. We can have a few hours together before the last flight leaves for London."

"Suit yourself," he replied flatly.

She followed Jacob down to his car and jumped into the passenger seat. She was still fighting to come to terms with how her afternoon had spun out of control from excitedly meeting Jacob at the airport to now when she found herself with the knowledge she knew would place her and her family in grave danger.

The drive to Odenton was a quiet one. Eventually they pulled up at Kevin's modest-but-neat home. The small front garden was well presented with trimmed grass. As they approached, they noticed the front door was ajar. Jacob turned to Alice who nodded before he pushed the door open and entered. Inside the house, it was a mess. They entered through the kitchen, which looked to them like it was being readied to be remodeled. Every drawer and cupboard had been ripped from its fasteners, the contents emptied on the floor. The main living area was no different; the smart LED TV had been torn from its wall mount, and the screen smashed and removed. Jacob walked slowly through the mess. The TiVo unit had been opened and its hard drive removed. The scene of destruction carried on up the stairs and into the two small bedrooms and bathroom. Alice took hold of Jacob's hand and squeezed it tightly.

"Do you think he's been burgled?" Alice asked nervously.

"No." Jacob answered quickly.

"I think we should leave Jacob."

They both knew what this was. If he'd been burgled they would have taken the TV, the TiVo and other items such as his PC, but they hadn't. Whoever did this had stripped the hard drives out of anything that had one. They were looking for something. Alice was right, they should leave.

But now he had a bigger question running through his mind. If they have found out that Kevin knew about the real reason for Martialis, it wouldn't take them anytime to connect Andy and himself. Still holding Alice's arm, he led her down the stairs, back out of the door they had entered through, and toward his Camry which was still parked at the kerb. *Thank God,* he thought to himself as they rushed toward it. He fumbled for the keys in his pocket and found them, pointing the small black fob at the car, he hit the unlock button and smiled.

He watched the indicators flash letting him know that the car was now open. Once inside they fastened their seatbelts and Jacob inserted the ignition key. As he turned it they both heard the bang. Jacob jumped in his seat and turned to Alice who was laughing at him. They heard it again; they both looked over to the street opposite, where a car was backfiring.

"That made you jump," she giggled.

Jacob didn't reply, it had made him jump and he was a little embarrassed by it. He smiled back at her and then turned the key. As the engine fired to life he spun the car around, retracing the route they had taken to get to Kevin's house, he started heading back toward Dulles.

"Where are you going?" Alice asked.

"Dulles; you need to be home and away from here."

"What about Andy?"

"After I've dropped you at Dulles I'll go to his house."

Jacob looked in his mirror and noticed a large black Chevrolet SUV behind them and he instantly knew who it was and what it meant. He also knew he couldn't allow that to happen. Not to Alice.

"We're being followed." Jacob warned her.

"Where?" Alice looked around and noticed the same car. "The black four-by-four?"

"Yes, I recognize the license plates. Government cars all use a certain pre-fix."

"How the hell did they get onto us this quick?" Alice sounded scared.

"Bruce and Jonathan were in on this, we know that. All they had to do was watch the rest of us. It wouldn't be that hard for them," Jacob answered.

"Now what? We pull over, plead ignorance?"

"No. If they've got Andy or Kevin, either of them may have told them I know, and now you're with me what do you think they'll do?" Jacob hit the steering wheel "Fuck!"

"What do we do?" Alice asked.

"In Australia, there is a small town east of Perth called Quairading. It's on the edge of the Badjaling Nature Reserve. If you change your mind and you want to spend the last few days with me, there is a community arts and resource center on Parker Street. Meet me there. Now listen to this bit carefully, there is a flight leaving Heathrow with four family members of Joe Jamison heading for Perth Airport. As I said, I have emailed you the official documents that will get you on that flight with your children. For some reason they're not numbered in anyway, so three will work as well as one. Once at Perth, Quairading is about two hours east, I need you to be there. I need you with me when it ends. Alice, please don't let me die alone."

Now sobbing, he turned and leaned across kissing her goodbye. She placed a hand tenderly on his cheek and whispered to him. "You won't be alone Jacob."

Still weeping he slung the steering wheel around. The Camry spun through 180 degrees. Jacob planted his foot hard onto the accelerator pedal. The three-litre engine responded and with all the power available, the Camry raced in the opposite direction of the black SUV. In one last attempt to lose them Jacob swerved, changing direction again, but the SUV stayed with them. Desperate, he allowed the SUV within a few feet of his rear bumper and then slammed on the brakes.

The jolt was painful as the trunk of the Camry took the full impact of the large Chevrolet, but it did what Jacob had hoped it would, with the SUV unbalanced Jacob slung the steering wheel to the left. As the Camry turned sharply, the Chevrolet flipped over landing heavily on the passenger side. Sliding uncontrollably, it hit a row of parked cars and came to a halt with steam hissing out of the smashed radiator. Jacob's Camry was now also coming to a stop. The impact had torn the gas tank from the floor of the trunk. With no fuel getting through to the engine, it coughed and spluttered to a stop.

Jacob slammed the dashboard. "Come on. We need to get out and get away on foot."

Holding her sore neck from the rear end shunt, Alice climbed out and joined Jacob. A few of the eyewitnesses were no doubt calling the police he thought to himself as they fled down a small ally, and onto the other side of the main street, which seemed almost deserted apart from a well-timed cab. Flagging it down, Jacob opened the door and pointed to Alice to get in, which she did.

"Remember what I told you, Quairading, Badjaling Nature Reserve. Don't go to your house. Call Rob from the plane. Make arrangements to meet him and the children. If you go home, they'll get you. You won't be safe in England. You need to hide out until you catch the plane. I'll see you in Australia."

Jacob kissed her one more time before he turned to the cab driver to give him the destination.

"Dulles Airport and quick."

Jacob watched as the taxi turned the corner. Once out of sight he made his way quickly to the bank across the street and withdrew his daily maximum from his checking account, and then from his three credit cards. He now had $6500 in cash to his name, and he knew this would be the last time he could use these cards. Growing up, he'd seen enough action and spy movies to know his cell would now be used to help his pursuers find him, and he would not be able to use his cards, so he pulled a pen from his pocket and wrote his pin number on each of the cards, then hailing down a taxi he got in. As the taxi set off he heard the first sirens that were no doubt responding to the SUV's crash

The cab driver headed toward the lower side of town. This wasn't the place you'd find a Jaguar or Porsche dealer, but it was just the place to find a cheap inconspicuous car, and where the dealer could be persuaded to lose the sales receipt and any trace of the transaction. The cab pulled up at a set of lights. With no cars around him and no CCTV, Jacob rolled down his window and dropped his bank card out of the car. A little farther he tossed out two of his credit cards, and a short while later, as the cab pulled up alongside the first, and typical road side used car lot, he put his cell under the rear seat and dropped the gold card from his pocket onto the sidewalk.

Smiling, he paid the cab driver and entered the lot.

Above him hung dirty tired advertising flags that at some point would have been bright and colorful, but over years they had become dull and tired, like the cars that were lined up under them. The small office to the rear of the lot had paint that was cracked and flaking, with what Jacob decided was a 1970's color theme of white over green, and the announcement speakers, no doubt put there in the days of multiple staff, hung off the rusty brackets with all but one of its wires cut, rendering it silent.

The cars were no better. Jacob hadn't been in a place like this since he'd bought his first car for $400, a faded red Saab. His Camry, bought by his dad, who sadly died soon after, was new out of the showroom only two years ago. But now it lay a wreck. What Jacob needed was an old car, not something so beat up it would attract the police, but not something too new. It was thirty minutes or so later when Jacob left as the latest owner of a silver 1996 Lincoln town-car. He fueled the car to the top, and bought a pre-paid cell phone. Pulling out of the forecourt he pointed the car north, and headed for Canada.

Back at Jacob's flat, the secured main entrance door flew open after it finally yielded to the hand-held battering ram, and in stepped four FBI agents and two local police officers, who were politely asked to remain outside the premises while his home was searched. As with Kevin's apartment, Jacob's was ransacked; every nook and cranny of the rented apartment was checked, draws, cupboards and cabinets were emptied. Any electrical item was taken as evidence, and his laptop and desk top PC were checked for their hard drives, but he'd taken them out before he had left with Alice and made sure he had them when he'd abandoned his Camry. Once they'd completed their search and found nothing of what they'd come for, one of the agents stepped outside and called his field office and spoke to the man they'd been seconded to, General Scott.

Agent Burton had been given the lead on apprehending Jacob. The team he'd sent to follow them had crashed their SUV, and two of them had been seriously injured. Burton had decided to search Jacob's home himself. And though he had not found what he came for, he'd taken some delight in wrecking the place.

"General Scott, this is Agent Burton. We're at Mr Miller's apartment now. I can confirm that while he has left his computers, he has taken the hard drives and destroyed the systems memory. He has also cleared his answer phone sir. I can confirm the journalist was here, we found a stained blouse in the trash and her laptop minus the hard drive. Has Agent Shaw apprehended her General?"

General Scott didn't welcome the news that no electronic or physical trail could be found. What made it worse still, was that Jacob, and Alice had managed to get away. His answer left agent Burton in no doubt. "No. He managed to get away, and that incompetent asshole Shaw managed to lose her at the airport. The only line of investigation we have is that he withdrew money from a bank. If he's stupid enough to do that once, then he'll do it again. And of course, we'll find him by his cell phone. He's switched it off, but we're working on activating it," General Scott answered.

"Okay sir. We'll return to the office and await any developments on the phone or cards. We should have him soon sir. Even government employees tend to panic. We're usually able to apprehend them within twelve hours. He'll be hiding somewhere close, perhaps a local motel. It's just a matter of time. I'm confident he's still in town. Just one more thing sir; I have sent undercover cars to stake out the friends and family he has had the most contact with over the last six months, just in case he pays them a visit. We will get him sir; of that I have no doubt," Agent Burton replied, hoping to calm the General.

General Scott didn't answer. Agent Burton returned to his car furious at being outplayed by Jacob. He sat behind the wheel and started the engine. "You win this one, but I'll find you," he whispered to himself as he pulled away.

Chapter 14
Heathrow Airport, London, United Kingdom

April 20th, 2023. 8:18 p.m. GMT.

Alice grabbed her luggage from the carousel and headed towards the *Europcar* desk, walking quickly. The information Jacob had given would have, at any other time in human history, brought down the U.S. President, and propelled her career to heights she could have only dreamt about. But this wasn't any other time in human history. It was the end of human history and of life on earth, and she knew once the announcements were made after the planned U.N. summit in a month's time civilization would break down, and running the story then or now wouldn't matter. Her only focus now was her children, she had to get home and get them to Australia. As she stood at the hire car desk two men in dark suits approached her. She felt sick with nerves, and her back became wet with the sweat which now ran down it. She picked up her luggage and began to turn, her paranoia now running amok in her mind.

As she took a step the first man blocked her. "Ms Fisher?" he said as he held out an I.D. Alice looked at it. The unmistakable badge read; MI6.

She gulped. "Yes, that's me," she answered.

"I'm intelligence officer Green. Please, come with us."

Alice turned and was flanked by the two men that led her into a small room behind the Virgin Atlantic check-in-desk. Inside was another man, but unlike the two that had escorted her, he was wearing only suit trousers and an open necked white shirt. His tie and jacket were thrown over one of the two chairs in the room.

"This is her," Green said.

The man nodded and gestured to Alice to sit. "Thank you," he said as Green and the other man left the room.

Alice sat nervously. She was used to dealing with people in power, but this was different. After the chase in DC, it was clear to her that they had interest in what Jacob had told her. But she also knew they couldn't know for sure what, if anything he had told her. And then the thought flashed into her mind. What if they had caught Jacob?

"Ms Fisher, I'm Mr Ford. My friends in MI6 have allowed me the courtesy of speaking to you."

Alice protested. "You know I'm a British Citizen, and we're on British soil?"

"Yes, and you know with the world going to shit in a little over a year, that doesn't matter now. Does it?"

Alice sank back in the chair.

"I'll come to the point, as you know time is fast running out. We know you were in contact with Jacob Miller yesterday and we know you went to see Kevin

Ricks. And I'm confident that if I had to guess you were on the way to see Andy Adams, but you spotted us and then, well, you know the rest."

"What's happened to Kevin? His house looked like a bomb had exploded."

"We have Kevin and Andy, and they're both fine. What we want now is Jacob."

"I don't know where he is, or where he's going."

"Here's the thing. You, Jacob Miller, Michael Forbes, Kevin Ricks and Andy Adams all have one thing in common. Do you know what that is, Ms Fisher?"

"No," Alice answered.

"You all know something that you weren't meant to know. You see you're all one big set, and we nearly have all the pieces."

"You have Michael too?" Alice asked.

"In a way."

"What does that mean? He is ok?" she asked.

"Unfortunately, Michael's car had an accident. It happens sometimes."

"Just who are you?" Alice asked.

"I've told you that Ms Fisher, you're stalling for time."

"You told me your name, not who you represent," she answered.

Mr Ford leant forward in his chair. "Where is Jacob going?"

"I've told you, I don't know."

"You do understand that you have committed treason against the United States of America?"

"Is that supposed to scare me? I'm in Britain, my editor knows I've landed, my husband knows I've landed, by the time you apply for extradition they'll be no United States of America left."

"You mean your ex-husband, don't you? Which leads to me to my next point."

"And what's that?" Alice swallowed hard as she answered him.

It was one thing being held by the FBI last year, and even being chased by them only yesterday. But this was different. Whoever this Mr Ford was, he was a different kind of man, the like of which Alice had not come across before. And he terrified her.

April 20th, 3:58 p.m. EST.
The Oval Office, The White House, Washington DC.

The small cell phone that sat in front of General Scott on the low coffee table began to ring. Bruce, Jonathan and President Young looked at the General as he took the call.

"General Scott speaking."

"General, it's Ford. I have Alice."

"And Miller?" General Scott asked.

"Not yet sir, he's running. But we'll get him," Ford answered.

The General hung up and put the cell phone back on the table. He turned to President Young.

"We have four out of five, sir," he said.

"Who's the missing piece?" President Young asked.

"Jacob Miller, but Ford said he'll have him soon," the General answered.

"Okay, Bruce I want you and Jonathan to relocate to the landing site in Australia. Keep us informed from there," President Young said.

"Yes sir," Jonathan answered.

As they left the President turned to General Scott. "Make sure they get Jacob Miller. If he opens up, this country will descend into chaos, and we have to consider how other countries will react if they find out we're responsible. With nothing to lose they could start an all-out nuclear attack," President Young said.

"We'll find him," the General assured him.

May 5th, 2023. 9:43 p.m. EST.
United Nations Plaza, New York.

After three weeks of meetings, negotiations and confirmations by each of the leaders own scientific advisory, an agreement had been reached on how and when each country would unilaterally broadcast and make public knowledge the details of the coming apocalypse, and how each country would take steps to slow the process and keep control of the populace. The world's leaders had been suspicious and skeptical when President Young had first presented to them what had been found in Resolute, and what it meant for all of the world's people and animals. Some countries had however been conspicuous by their absence and refusal to attend the summit. But it would always be the case those countries which isolated themselves from the western developed world would always see what was happening through suspicious eyes. North Korea especially had been noticeable by their absence, choosing to withdraw even more from then rest of the world. Some Islamic and African countries had also withdrawn, blaming the western way of life for the catastrophe that would now prove once and for all if there was a God, and if an afterlife paradise awaited. But while they blamed the west, their accusations were based on the traditional reasons of hatred: a difference of religion or way of life. If they knew the truth behind the anomaly, their distrust and hatred would prove to be finally justified. But Jacob had disappeared. General Scott was unable to throw the resources he wanted into finding him, the U.S. military was being recalled from around the world ready to be placed in towns and cities across the U.S. to keep order when the announcements were made. And so far, Ford had always been two steps behind him.

It was the last night of the scheduled meetings, and time for the countries in the northern hemisphere was running out. Already the northern territories of Canada had been enveloped. Resolute was now an abandoned ghost town, as was any populated area on the same latitude. These areas had been evacuated on the back of some story about poisoning and an environmental catastrophe. The few people that did refuse to leave had now perished. After leaving the UN Plaza, President Young was driven by armored motorcade to his Presidential Helicopter which would take him onto the White House. Tonight, it was an especially somber journey. The time to inform the world's population had now been agreed, in what now seemed no time at all, this situation had gone from a discussion in the Oval Office to a summit unlike the world had not been seen before, and would never see again. But for President Young the announcement to the American people made it official and from that moment on, any hopes or dreams of it being a mistake would be gone forever. The date agreed for the world to change for everyone had been set for June 1st, eighteen hundred hours GMT. Leading up to that date all cell phones, email addresses and chat accounts would be sent a message with the time and date of the announcement, and all TV channels, radio stations and internet channels would carry the same message simultaneously.

As thoughts of what was coming spun through his head, the President's helicopter landed on the south lawn of the White House. He climbed down the small steps and walked wearily into the venerable building that had become a beacon of light and hope across the U.S. and to many other people around the world. Surrounded by his bodyguards and the military, he made straight for his private quarters.

The following morning President Young sat in the Oval Office. All the official trips, talks and conferences had been cancelled. It seemed obvious now that the President needed to be confined to the White House for security. He sat staring out of the large windows and across the landscaped gardens, thinking of the great men and women throughout history who had graced the building and had sat at this seat, making decisions that shaped the United States.

"Abraham, what would you do if you were alive today? How would you do it? Could you have stopped it? Is there something we're missing? Something so obvious and stupid no one dares to propose it? God, if there is someone out there who has such an idea please send that person forward." His impromptu prayer was interrupted by his private aid knocking on the heavy door and then entering with an official sealed document.

"This has just been delivered. They told me you must see it alone and immediately, sir."

"Thank you, Gary." President Young took the sealed envelope from him.

Alone, he pulled open the large sealed envelope and slid out the documents.

He looked at the front cover and paused before he opened it. He knew inside were the final decisions that he, along with the Joint Chiefs and Vice President, had come to in what would eventually prove to be a futile effort to save the United States. But he also appreciated they had to do something to try and fight it. It was in the DNA of every animal to fight to the last, to keep trying, even in the face of insurmountable odds. But he also recognized that some of the decisions made to allow a fight back had been made with a heavy heart and some it seemed without a heart at all. Decisions based on pure logic and not sympathy or empathy, if these decisions were carried out, could it be said that sometimes the most human thing to do is to accept defeat, to lay down your arms and find peace with yourself before the end comes.

He opened the glossy cover and began to read.

CONFIDENTIAL

In Summary: The steps agreed to maximize America's oxygen before the country is ultimately asphyxiated and the population is overcome by suffocation.

1: Details of the first steps to be taken:

Anything that relies on a combustion process to produce power will need oxygen to help feed that process, it is therefore a sensible procedure to limit the use of such facilities, for that reason the following rules would come into force.

1.   Only emergency and military services would be allowed to use any kind of vehicle, all non-emergency and domestic vehicles will be under a strict curfew of non-use which would be enforced by armed police and armed forces. Any vehicles seen would be stopped and the engines destroyed.

2.   All power stations that produce power by burning fossil fuels or recycled fuel sources should be shut down, only nuclear-powered stations would continue to produce electricity, all power would be diverted to essential buildings first. What is left will then be divided through rolling blackouts.

3.   All trains, shipping and air transport will cease. All non-essential public services will be closed, only the highest emergencies will be responded to.

4.   Curfews for the population will be put in place to keep the streets clear. This will prevent attacks on people and stop the possibility of riots starting. The times people will be allowed out will be determined by their address within a zip code and will be managed by the local police or military commanders on the ground.

5.   Manufacturing will cease in all sectors.

6.   Gas supply will stop nationwide to stop the use of domestic burners, boilers. Air conditioning units will also be classed as non-essential and no longer allowed to be used. Private generators will be classed as illegal as they use a combustion process.

Secondary steps: Recommendations of actions to be taken to maximize available oxygen levels for as long as will be possible.

1.   All domestic animals or non-essential animals will be culled. This includes all animals classed as pets of any species and breed, only animals needed for control will be excused. Other animals to be culled will include all zoo animals and wild animals that can be easily hunted.

2.   People on life support and the long term terminally ill will be assessed individually, as will all prisoners on death penalties and life sentences.

3.   Anybody found looting or acting in a violent way will be terminated by the authorities in charge of that area.

4.   Any new born children that require ventilation care or medical intervention will receive no such care allowing for a natural death.

5.   All...

President Young slammed the document shut, enraged by what he had in front of him, his eyes swollen with tears. How had we fallen so far and so fast? Laying out in detail the people in society that should be given life or denied it made him sick to his core, and was against everything he believed in. He had no right to decide these things. Is a world that imposes such barbaric measures, just to extend its own life worth saving while we choose not to keep those alive that need it the most? Throughout human history it was always the most vulnerable that bore the brunt of the decisions made by those who thought it their right to lead and to decide the fate of others. If humankind was to end, then it would not end with the death of the innocent. He would not go to his own death with that on his conscience, and while it had seemed the logical thing to extend the majority of lives, he saw clearly now it was also the wrong thing to do. To be human is not to be logical; it is to be sympathetic. It is to have empathy and love in your heart for others, and especially for those in greater need than yourself.

There would be law and order of course, but he would not allow this once great nation to decay into a totalitarian regime of absolute power and absolute corruption of the human condition. He turned to his computer and logged into the main server. From there he found the file directory that held the electronic version of what he had on his desk.

He highlighted it and with no hesitation, but with a sense of complete righteousness, he pressed the delete key. Now he'd reminded himself of what it meant and felt to be human.

But his sense of calm soon left him. It wasn't long before what he had done was noticed, and his phone began to ring.

"Mr President. The file for the guidelines has been deleted off the system, we can't get it back, we may have been hacked sir."

Jonathan sounded panicky on the phone. President Young smiled to himself and then reassured him. "It is fine Jonathan. I have decided we are not going to implement the full plan, and I have deleted it, and furthermore, I want physical copies destroyed."

The relief was almost tangible down the phone line as Jonathan sighed.

"Thank God for that sir, for both sir, I mean for not doing it and that we're not being hacked sir."

"That's fine Jonathan, and thank you."

President Young called in his private secretary and dictated a memorandum that was to be sent to everyone on the newly created email directory that dealt with the coming event, and it said only this.

"I have decided that we as a nation are not going to set in motion events which once started cannot be stopped or reversed. Therefore, operations Diutinus and Sustineo will no longer be initiated in their original formats. All documents detailing these operations, must be destroyed. This is a Presidential order. I will personally give details of steps to be taken within the next forty-eight hours."

With the memo finished he thanked his secretary and asked for it to be finished in the usual way. President Young stretched and sighed. He had the feeling this was going to be a long and difficult day. More than that he knew the coming days were going to become much, much worse.

May 25th, 2023. 11:35 a.m. UTC-3. Halifax Stanfield International Airport, Nova Scotia. Canada.
(During Canada's final days)

Jacob had spent his days since fleeing the U.S. sleeping in his car or staying in out-of-the-way motels. He'd hoped that the dropped bank cards would have had the agents seconded to General Scott busy on a wild goose chase. He'd hoped that writing his pin number on the cards would make it easy enough for the people who found them to withdraw money and use the cards in shops. While the agents were busy tracking them, Jacob had slipped away, and leaving his phone in the back of the cab had kept them busy for a day. Jacob didn't need money, and no one would when the anomaly arrived. He hoped whoever had used his cards had at least enjoyed themselves while it had lasted. But now he had to fly. He had to get to Heathrow, London to be able to fly onto Perth.

He knew that the agents working for General Scott would have their eyes at every airport that offered a flight to the UK. But he'd gambled that as Canada approached the estimated date when it would longer be habitable, the chances of them continuing their stake out of airports this far north would stop. He also gambled that by flying to Australia via the U.K would also throw them off. He was certain with the limited man power they would have now, they would only be checking the direct flights. This was why he'd waited.

He had enough money for an onward flight from Canada to Australia in his pocket and little extra. Somewhat bedraggled and with a good growth of facial hair, he slowly pulled the car that had been his home for the last few weeks into the multi-story parking structure. Ensuring that he parked on the second level, he reversed it in to a corner parking bay and switched off the engine. He sat for a while looking directly out of the windshield at the neatly parked rows of cars in front of him. He tried to imagine what this place would like after a month, a year, and a decade. During his brief stops in road side diners he'd seen the news reports as people panicked, fleeing the invisible death that now stalked its way down. Creeping slowly south, killing everything that failed to get ahead of it. For the most part people still believed it was some sort of environmental disaster. But he appreciated that wouldn't hold for much longer. But then, it didn't need to. It had always been the plan to delay the announcement until the last possible minute. It made sense to evacuate the government first, to get them out of the White House and even out of the country, before widespread panic set in. But he didn't know where it was, he hadn't been allowed that information. Blinking to get the haunting image out of his mind he stepped out of the car leaving the keys in the ignition.

He would have no further use of this car, but if someone saw the keys in it and it gave them one last chance to flee then he wished them well. He hoped that the car would prove as useful to them as it had to him. As he walked through the airport it hit him how empty and quiet it was. The southbound lanes of the highways had been packed as people had started to abandon the northern countries. He'd almost had the northbound lane to himself.

He made his way to the closest flight desk where he imagined he would be able to buy a ticket for the journey he needed to make. He was met politely by a pleasant slim woman wearing the red white and blue uniform of British Airways.

Jacob approached her smiling as best he could with his unkempt appearance. He would shave and make himself presentable only when he was on the flight from London to Perth. Reassuring himself, he couldn't possibly imagine that General Scott would pursue him to Australia. By then the announcement would have taken place. There would be no need to keep him quiet, and besides, they would have their hands full.

"Hi," Jacob said as he approached the desk, and then continued "I need to get a connecting flight to Perth Australia, stopping in the UK. Can I get one here?"

She checked her computer screen. Jacob had no idea what she was looking at on the screen. He imagined now she was flagging the agents and that at any moment they would put a heavy hand on his shoulder and whisper *'Come with us sir'* and of course that would mean no one would see him again, but to his delight and absolute relief no hand appeared, just a polite smile from *Becky*.

"Yes sir, we have a flight leaving at one o'clock this afternoon from gate two. Do you have luggage sir?" she asked.

"Only carry on," he said trying to remain calm. Playing it cool had never been Jacob's strong suit, which is why he'd only ever played poker once.

"Okay sir, in standard class the cost is three thousand, three hundred and seventy-nine dollars U.S. sir. Should I go ahead and book it?"

"That's fine, that's one ticket? That guarantee's me to Perth is that correct?" he had to be sure.

"Yes sir. You have two changes; one at Heathrow London, and then one in Hong Kong. It's a nine-hour layover in London and two hours in Hong Kong."

Jacob was shaken a little at the thought of the layover in London, but he had no choice. He didn't know when the announcement would be made, but when it was, pandemonium would set in, and where ever he was, he would likely be stuck there.

"That's fine, I'll take it. I'll pay cash."

Jacob pulled a large envelope from his jacket and started to count out the fare, hoping with all his being that Becky wouldn't be alarmed and call ahead. Spending this much money and then paying in cash always arose suspicion of drug running and money laundering, but again, he had no choice. He finished counting and smiled at her with his best, *I'm honest, nothing to be distrustful about here please don't call anyone* smile. She turned back to the computer and started hitting the keys again.

"As you're paying by cash sir I just need you to fill in this form for proof of I'D, its standard procedure sir," she said as she handed it to him.

He took the form off her, and felt his hand shake as he did. *What the fuck do I do now?* He thought to himself. He could put a false name down? But then if she asked to see his driver license or passport she'd know instantly. Perhaps the agents hadn't told this airport to watch out for him. They may have thought he'd use a U.S. airport. Maybe they thought he was still in the U.S. They didn't know that he had a reason to leave, and especially from Canada to Australia. The thoughts rushed through his head, tumbling around, confusing him. He felt that everybody and every camera was looking directly at him, and that hand on his shoulder would come at last, but his thoughts of final defeat here in this airport were brought to a sudden stop by Becky.

"Sir, are you okay? I'll also need to see your passport." he asked him.

That was it; he had no way now of lying on the form. He had to give his true details. Clenching his teeth together he filled in the form, giving the correct name; address, and date of birth. It was as if he was completing his own arrest warrant. Apprehensively he gave her the form and his passport and waited for the alarms to sound. His legs twitched, full of adrenaline, ready to run, to sprint as fast as his legs could, then he thought about the car keys. *Why did I leave the fucking keys in the car, I may need it to get away, shit!*

"Here's your receipt, passport and tickets with the details of the transfers and lay overs. Have a good journey. Thank you for choosing British Airways," Becky said as she handed it all to him.

Jacob took the items from her, nodding to her in appreciation. His heart continued to pound in his chest. All he had to do now was get through passport control, and he would be a step closer to freedom, and to Alice. He walked through the airport toward gate two. He duly arrived at passport control and handed it over to the gentleman behind the desk. He, unlike Becky, didn't look fresh faced and easy going. Rather, he looked like ex-police or ex-military, and Jacob smiled nervously, trying to keep his new state of relaxation. But he felt it collapsing quickly back to a state of panic and dread. The state he'd spent the last few months of his life in.

Time stood still. He had all but given up, nearly deciding to turn himself in. What did it matter anyway? They would all be dead in a matter of months. Jacob sighed as the ex-policeman handed him back his passport and nodded him through. He'd made the first part. He could now board the aircraft. But he still couldn't relax.

May 26th, 2023. 6:27 p.m. EST. The Oval Office, The White House. Washington DC

President Benjamin Young sat behind his desk. As time moved on, and the hand of the world's clock came closer to the day of the announcement, the more surreal it all seemed. Jonathan and Bruce had done everything they could, and were now in Australia, monitoring the anomaly as it continued its crawl south. The rift for now, thankfully, was holding steady. General Scott walked into the office and stood in front of his desk.

"It's time, sir," General Scott said.

"Already? Let me just have a minute, General."

"Yes, sir. I'll be outside the door."

"Just before you go." The President stopped the General from leaving. "Do you think we did the right thing?"

General Scott looked at him inquisitively, unsure of what the President was referring to.

"About Kevin, Andy and Michael. Do you think we handled it correctly?" The President asked.

"Yes sir. We did. We had to take measures to protect the secret Mr President. If Kevin had let it become common knowledge of what we did, and why this is happening, well I'm afraid to think of how the world, and our own citizens, would have reacted."

"And what are the plans for Kevin and Andy?" President Young asked.

"We do not have the man power now to incarcerate threats from liabilities such as them sir. Under the anti-terrorism act following nine-eleven sir, section eighteen of the act gives me the powers to seconder agents from the FBI, CIA and homeland security. To make sure that no threats to the American way of life are allowed to continue once identified sir. And that means by any action needed. Sir."

President Young bowed his head and sighed before responding to General Scott. "Very well. If that's how it has to be."

"It is, sir," General Scott said somewhat subdued, but his job right now was to take President Young to the rendezvous point at the Oceana Naval Air squad base Virginia. "Sir, we have to leave, we have no time left."

President Young nodded and left the office that throughout history had been witness to some of the greatest decisions ever made by mankind. But he'd sadly witnessed some of the worst as well. It was hard for President Young as he left the White House for the last time. He was heavy with the knowledge he would be the last President, and that he could not say goodbye to any of his faithful staff, some of whom had been with him since his earliest days in politics.

The waiting Presidential helicopter lifted from the White House lawn. He always preferred this view. The White House at night shone like a symbol of hope in the darkness, a place of promise and safety in an ever-changing world. But soon it was out of sight, he was now heading for what was to be his new and final home.

Chapter 15

After it was realized what was to come, and it became clear and accepted that nothing could reverse it, a plan to maintain a working U.S. Government had been planned and put into place. The best place for any chance of survival would be deep underwater. The U.S. Navy had retrofitted four of its Ohio-class nuclear submarines, the largest submarines the Navy had ever built. By taking out the weapons that made them perhaps the most devastating war machine designed by men and fitting them out to maintain a working government the President's sub, aptly named Sea-Force One, would be home for the President; his family, closest aides and advisers and staff. The front of the sub had been fitted with living accommodation and offices; further back was a complete replica of the White House briefing room, from where the broadcast would be made. This gave the American public and foreign leaders, as well as the UN, the illusion that the President had not left the White House. The second sub held the Vice President and his family and staff; the third sub carried the joint chiefs, their families and staff. The crew had been specially selected to ensure they were a fifty-fifty male-to-female split of heterosexuals from all the available ethnic backgrounds the Navy could muster. And the usual rules of no fraternization had been lifted. The reason was simple. To repopulate a planet with a strong viable population you need one hundred-sixty people, eighty breeding pairs. And the easiest way to achieve this would be to allow the crew to form relationships and to start procreating. Some of the crew were already married or in relationships. But all of them, without exception, were childless. For this reason, sub four was largely empty, and would in due course become the home for the children, who in turn would be trained in various areas of expertise the new world would need. But one thing would be very different for this generation. No religion would play a part in their lives. Escorting these four subs were six fully armed and crewed hunter killer class, and another two fully armed Ohio-class submarines. During the previous months, the U.S. Navy had been placing caches of food, parts, air and weaponry around the world in some of the deepest oceans in purpose-made pods. The subs could dock with these pods using the lower air locks. This small fleet would hold the last survivors of the Human Race and had the ability to remain submerged for a period of six years. The hope was simple, that by then the magnetosphere would have repaired itself, allowing the subs to make for what was once the United States of America.

This was a secret that even the closest advisors and staff had not been told. Unless that is, they were to be part of the President's staff on board one of the subs. As the helicopter landed, President Young saw the submarine. Its black shape loomed out of the covered dock side. Only parts of the glistening black hull were visible inside this huge launching hangar which stopped any spy satellites from being able see it.

Slowly he boarded it, knowing this would, in all probability, be the last time he would feel the soil of his beloved country beneath his feet. He entered the belly of the metal leviathan where he was met by the captain and his XO. All the submarines in the armada had only the best captains and crew. The President made his way through the sub until he reached the door that said *Presidential personnel only allowed beyond this point.* Next to it stood two armed guards both of whom saluted the President as he made his way through the door, and into what was now his home, and place of work for at least as long as they either needed to stay under water, or had the ability to stay under water, regardless of the surface conditions.

As he walked into his private quarters he was greeted by his family. He was so relieved to see them both safe and on board, he didn't notice the small noise and vibration as the submarine embarked, ready to join the already submerged fleet waiting two nautical miles from the base. As the fleet began to head away from the coast to begin to dive to depths, from which they could not be tracked, the future for those on board was no more certain than for those left on land.

June 1st, 2023. 6:00 p.m. GMT

Every TV and radio station streamed internet video, and every other form of communication, visual or audible of every nation, flickered and then presented their countries leader, elected or not. The message that spelled out the end for those watching or listening had been agreed by everyone at the summit. That one single message would go to all the peoples of the world, regardless of religion, beliefs or nationalities. The world's news stations had received prior notice of the broadcast so they could build it into their schedule. Even so, like the people watching, they had no idea of what the content was.

In the United States President Benjamin Young could be seen on every screen and heard on every radio.

"To all my fellow Americans, and more importantly my fellow human beings, regardless of where you are or who you are. Today, as this country's leader, it is my duty to bring news that I wished with all my heart I did not have to. An event has taken place that is already starting to affect the planet on which we live. The sun that has provided the earth and every creature on it with life has experienced a massive and previously unthought-of Coronal Mass Ejection. This ejection of plasma carried trillions of tons of debris which hit our magnetosphere and fatally damaged it. Because of that event a rift has formed in the southern hemisphere which has caused a vacuum on earth. This anomaly is spreading south from the northern hemisphere. This vacuum is exactly the same as that which is experienced in space. And the resulting increase in size means that eventually the earth itself will become uninhabitable by July next year. It is to my regret that life in the United States will have ended by late September this year. So, what can we do to avert this coming catastrophe? Well, the simple fact is we can't stop it but we can delay it. Which is why I am announcing that from midnight tonight all private forms of transport that require the use of oxygen, such as gas and diesel powered' vehicles, will no longer be allowed to be in use. All power stations that use a combustion process to produce power will be powered down and shut off. All public transport will cease to run in seven days. This time is to allow anyone away from home to get back. This is except for all internal flights which will be grounded from nine a.m. tomorrow morning. All international flights will be unilaterally grounded on June 5th. Now listen to me carefully, there will be no profiteering from this. The price you paid for milk today will remain the same until it is no longer available. I have ordered troops to work with the police to ensure that peace remains with us. Riots and public disorder or crime of any kind will be dealt with quickly and under the rules of martial law. This vacuum, this thing that is advancing across our great country that will eventually consume the earth cannot be stopped or hidden from."

The President paused as he wiped a tear from his eye. "This will be my final broadcast, I wish you all peace and prayers regardless of your beliefs and religion. It seems now that as our days on this planet come have to an end, we can all find a common belief. The differences that have caused so many wars and spilled so much blood, separating families and causing pain in the worst ways we know, now bond us together in a common purpose. That is to help and support our neighbors before that final part of life becomes a reality. God speed to you all, and may peace be with you."

President Young stood from behind the mocked-up desk inside the submarine, there was no turning back now that most of the world's population; rich or poor, famous or not, knew what was coming and what it meant for all life. He made his way through to his quarters to be with his family, the one place now he would find peace to keep the demons that haunted his sleep, and his waking hours away. He sat next to Samantha. She took him into her arms and the man that was once the most powerful man on earth sobbed for all of mankind, and for his own child.

Even at this depth there were no guarantees. Those aboard the submarine appreciated they would not be immune. No one knew for certain what would happen to the seas. They knew the oxygen could be drawn from them, but not at what rate or what effect that would have on sea levels, tides, or the strength of the current. It was all guess work. It was all they had. They knew that among the sea creatures it would be the mammals that would be the first to perish: whales, dolphins and other air breathing sea life, along with all life at the surface. But what effect it would have on the bottom dwellers that spend their entire life in the pitch-black cold of the deepest seas was all guess work. It might be that once again, life would start in the seas first and then make the transition to life on land, but that would of course depend completely on whether the magnetosphere was able to repair itself.

Across the world now families watched and listened as the news anchors that had delivered their daily news now responded to the announcements. With the coming curfews and ban on civilian transport people left what they were doing and began the journey home. Business people abandoned meetings and headed back to their cars, or the airports, or the train stations. Those that had heard the broadcast on their car radios had to stop, shell shocked and in denial. Highways came to a standstill as strangers got out of their cars and spoke to people they would normally only pass without so much as a second thought. They were looking for confirmation, not of what they'd heard, they were desperate to be wrong, what they wanted was confirmation they'd misunderstood the message. But none came.

Teachers sent children home, factories ground to halt as all across the world people walked out of their work place. In the most holy places on earth people began praying. Those who had prayed all of their lives were joined by those who had never prayed. In other areas as the shock started to give way to panic, people began raiding shops for food, water, batteries and anything they could grab and carry or push into a shopping cart. The human world had begun its collapse. And it wouldn't end with a whimper; it would end with seven billion voices crying out into the darkness of the universe.

Kevin and Andy had been held in the same cell since the day they'd been arrested. Andy was awake when he heard the heavy door that separated their cell block from the main corridor open. He leant across and nudged Kevin, who was asleep.

"Kevin, wake up. They're coming," he whispered.

Kevin had barely opened his eyes when their cell door was opened. Two guards entered, both armed with assault rifles.

"Stand and face the back wall and put your hands behind your heads," the first guard ordered.

Kevin and Andy had been through this routine before. Next, they expected to feel the cuffs being clasped over their wrists.

"You're moving us again?" Andy asked.

"Something like that," the guard replied.

Kevin heard the click he was expecting, but this wasn't the same sound the handcuffs had made before. As he looked at Andy who was standing to his left, he heard another sound. At the instant he heard it, Andy's forehead exploded. As Kevin turned to plead for his life, and urine ran down his legs, another shot rang through the cell block. By the time the sound had faded. Kevin and Andy were dead.

August 28th, 2023. 11:17 a.m. Local Time.
The Badjaling Nature Reserve.

The families of the returning astronauts took their position to watch the SOL 1 capsule return to earth. The main body of the ship had split from the propulsion unit when it had achieved a low earth orbit eight days ago. They'd had to wait until the weather was calm enough to attempt a landing at the impromptu runway, while the main propulsion would stay in orbit for a further forty-eight hours before starting a two-year journey to the sun where it would burn up and be consumed long before it would hit the surface.

After the decision had been made that a landing at Florida was not possible, the nature reserve in Australia had been chosen. The land was flattened to allow the astronauts and lander a relatively smooth and safe landing. The Australian Government had restricted the flow of people into the country immediately they'd heard of the anomaly. Knowing that people would flee south their warships patrolled the waters, turning back any boats that tried to cross from the South-East Asia. And any that didn't turn back they sank. After the unilateral air travel embargo the Royal Australian air force turned back any unauthorized aircraft that tried to enter their airspace, whether it was civil, personal or military. But even so they didn't want to risk landing the shuttle at a regular airport. If the shuttle had crashed and damaged the runways, it would shut an airport down for good. The idea of the nature reserve was adopted instead.

The shuttle could now be seen by the naked eye as it passed through the atmosphere and high cloud cover: the only blot on this day when the sky was a deep summer blue.

The lander came closer; its brilliant silver body work now glinted in the strong Australian sun. As it finally touched down plumes of reddish-brown dust were thrown up and instantly turned into vortices that swirled as they left the edge of the small wings. Family members and NASA staff, as well as Bruce and Jonathan watched with immense relief as it stopped at the end of the runway, near to where the small crowd had gathered. A few moments later the side airlock opened and the three-man crew exited. A round of applause followed instantly the moment Jake, Chun and Sergey could be seen. Their families rushed toward them, including the families of Mary and Joe, who were keen to find out if their loved ones were in good health. And to get answers, to help them understand their decision to stay on Mars. Maybe there was something else, something that had been said or that NASA had not told them, but Jake and Sergey assured their families that they were both fine, that there were no hidden reasons why they wanted to stay. The fact was, they just did. In those last few months of uncertainties, a simple and uncomplicated reason was a refreshing change and one that Joe and Mary's loved ones grasped at.

The NASA staff, astronauts, and their families slowly ambled away from the landing site, and as the engineers carried out the final shut down procedures, the sun started its decent. SOL 1 would be left where it had landed. There were no plans to move it, why would there be? It wouldn't matter where it was in a few short months. The engineers had sealed the ship. No one could now gain access. After all, it was designed to withstand the worst storms Mars could throw at it, and travel through space.

The ship had helped mankind achieve its greatest goal of reaching Mars. The planet which all astronomers had gazed on with wonder, the planet that had spawned so much pop culture and science fiction and had fascinated every culture on earth. With the astronauts now with their families, Bruce and Jonathan rendezvoused with Sea-Force One from there they would be able to continue monitoring the anomaly and the rift.

September 30th, 2023. On board Sea-Force One.

Confirmation reached President Young that the United States of America was no more. Everything in his beloved country was now enclosed by the vacuum. The anomaly had now passed over it. All that the country had endured, all of its history, from the native people, to the first settlers, from there to being the wealthiest and most powerful country on earth, was now consigned to history.

Along with North America, Northern Europe too had fallen, as had the Scandinavian countries and Northern Russia. The President called for a two-minute silence so that the crew of their small fleet could mourn for the United States and the people of our dying planet. Outside, the dark freezing cold water passed over the submarine's hulls as the secret fleet lay hidden in the depths of the Marianas Trench.

October 3rd, 2023.

Jacob had landed in Australia on May 27th. Since then he had hidden, exchanging his U.S. dollars for Australian dollars. He'd stayed hidden until the northern hemisphere was locked deep inside the vacuum. Now he knew it was, he no longer believed he would be followed. As far as he was concerned, President Young, General Scott and Bruce had perished when the United States had succumbed. He'd received a call from Alice three days after they'd escaped the FBI pursuit. She had told him that she would make to Australia, and that she would meet him where he had said to on this date at 2 p.m. outside the arts center. He was ready, and he was excited, he would finally get to be with her. Jacob tried to find faith since he'd arrived here. His knowledge of science and the rules of physics had given him so much and so many answers that he could never turn his back on it. But now in this time, when he needed it most, when he needed it to explain why this was happening, what the future would hold, if anything, and what would happen to him when he died had abandoned him, leaving him far more questions than answers and this confused and angered him. Why couldn't he figure this out? There could be only one conclusion, and that was no one was supposed to.

He had heard that the most intelligent people cannot use all their potential brain power. If this was the case, did someone or something keep us from experiencing what it would be like to use all of our intelligence? With this answer stuck in an everlasting loop, the only conclusions he could reach forced him to reconsider the beliefs he'd held all his life, and it seemed he'd been wrong. It became clear to Jacob now that science was man's invention it was nothing more than us making answers to fit the questions, sometimes in the most ludicrous way. There was only one thing that answered his questions at once, and fitted them all, tied them all up, leaving no gaps or areas of doubt. Jacob believed now that only God could achieve all that had been since the birth of the cosmos, that science was nothing more than God himself giving us the tools to answer the questions we needn't even have asked.

But now it was too late, mankind's quest to ignore this simple revelation, to control and master all we saw had resulted in us creating our own end. It wouldn't be the wrath of God that brought about the apocalypse. It would be our own greed, our own selfishness at not being satisfied with this Eden that God had provided for us. Jacob was clear minded now, he would welcome God into his heart, and he knew to do that he'd also have to welcome the end. He would do that with Alice by his side. He could think of no one he'd rather be with when the world ended.

All he had to do now was make it to Quairading and find Alice waiting for him at the community arts college. Smiling to himself that he'd beaten the system that tried to keep him in the U.S. he headed toward the row of waiting cabs. With the last $250 he had to his name, he climbed into the back of the first cab he came upon.

"The arts center in Quairading please."

The cab driver started driving toward the small town.

"I'm surprised to see you working what with everything coming to an end." Jacob remarked.

"Ya gotta mate. The government made it perfectly clear that life would proceed as normal. The sneaky buggers put troops everywhere to make sure it would too, look, the bloody bastards are all over the place. Anyway mate, what else we gotta do, sit around at home with the wife, and wait for it? Not on your nelly mate."

Jacob smiled, not only at the colorful description the cab driver had given him, but the way in which life here seemed to be almost normal. He sat back and watched the view from his window change from metropolitan city, to suburbs and finally to the Outback. The two hours went by quicker than he thought they would, and after his outburst the cabby had become silent. Jacob dozed off for a much-welcomed sleep. He was woken by a pothole in the road. As his eyes focused and he once again became used to the glaring afternoon sun, his heart lifted when he saw the sign which said *Welcome to Quairading.* The cab carried on a little further and eventually pulled up on Perth Street, directly outside the arts center as Jacob had requested during one brief discussion before he'd fallen asleep.

He thanked, and paid the cab driver, who he watched drive away before checking his pockets. $65.00 left to his name, but it didn't matter, money meant nothing now, at least not to him. As always though there were people making profits from mankind's suffering, but the cab driver didn't look to be one of them. Perhaps the cabby took the money in a desperate attempt to keep things as normal as he could, and maybe that was why he was working at all? Whatever the reason, Jacob quickly pushed the thought process from his mind. instead filling it with the image that Alice would soon walk around the corner, and as in some Hollywood love film their last few months would be happy, and would hold no room for life's regrets.

Almost precisely as he'd imagined it, Alice did emerge from the arts center. She stood now only ten meters away and Jacobs's heart lifted. With his newfound faith and the one woman he had ever truly loved standing before him he felt now that his life was complete. As he took a step towards her, he saw her expression change. A sadness filled her eyes and his mind scrambled to make sense of it. Alice's children stepped out behind her, followed by Rob. Jacob stopped and looked at her, and then to her family, before looking back to Alice. His heart sank as she slowly and discreetly shook her head, signaling for him to keep away.

Motionless and with a tear rolling down his face, he watched as she turned and walked away, her arm around Rob's waist and her two boys walking beside her.

As she turned the corner and Jacob lost sight of her, he felt an impact between his shoulder blades as if someone had hit him a baseball bat. He spun around but saw no one. As he stood trying to make sense of it he felt a burning sensation where the impact had hit him, and then a scorching pain radiate out. His breathing became irregular and panic started to rise up inside him. Another hit, this time the left side of his naval. Now he felt a warm wet sensation run down his side from where the pain was. He put his hand inside his shirt and pulled it back out, it was covered in his blood, and he realized he'd been shot.

Another hit, this time in his chest. Jacobs legs buckled, and he fell to his knees, his breathing became tight and contracted and painful. Falling backward he landed heavily and his arms flopped by his side. His body was still trying to give him the strength he needed to flee to safety, but it was futile and Jacob felt his life seeping from the wounds. His breathing was now fast and shallow, he turned his head but his vision was fading.

He made out two shadows standing over him. Jacob raised his right arm, holding his hand to them as he asked for help, but none came. As everything went black and he could feel the last few shallow breaths escape his body, he heard the shadows talking.

"Tell General Scott this is Mr Ford. We have taken care of Jacob. We're bringing Alice, and her family with us as agreed. We're heading back to rendezvous with the subs."

Eight months earlier: April 20th, 2023. 8:18p.m. GMT. Heathrow Airport, London, United Kingdom.

"You mean your ex-husband, don't you? Which leads to me to my next point."

"And what's that?" Alice swallowed hard as she answered him.

"Either you give up Jacob Miller Ms Fisher, or we hold you. And that Audi Q3 your ex-husband drives your children around in, will suffer the same electrical failure that Michael Forbes' Range Rover did." Mr Ford sat back in his chair.

Alice shook with fear. She had no choice. It was Jacob or her family.

"Okay, I'll tell you, but if he means so much to you, I want some guarantee, some security for my family."

Mr Ford smiled. "We can keep you safe, alive even after this anomaly has covered the earth. We know all about you Alice, we can use someone like you. But you have to give us Jacob."

"I'm meeting him on October 3rd, in Australia outside an arts center. A town called Quairading, it's near Perth."

Alice sighed. She hated herself right now. But she had to protect her family.

"You're free to go Ms Fisher, don't go to work, call in tomorrow and quit. And take that flight to Australia." Mr Ford said as he stood, and left the room.

January 15th, 2024. Sea-Force One. 11:38 a.m. GMT.

Bruce entered the briefing room where he found President Young and Jonathan waiting for him. The earth was now completely exposed to the vacuum of space as the previous year had drawn to a close the rift had gained exponentially in size accelerating the anomaly. The people in the southern hemisphere were taken by surprise believing they had a few months left, they were not as ready as they should have been. Perhaps it was the last cruel hand to be played by the universe, to give someone a false hope and then snatch it away before they have prepared themselves fully.

Christmas and New Year had not been celebrated on board the fleet of subs. It seemed to all the crew that there was nothing to celebrate. The notion of religion had by-and-large been abandoned in the face of what was happening above them. How could a God as loving as the Christian God, allow such suffering? Even if it is to be believed that he would punish mankind again as he has in the pages of the Bible. Why would he punish all the other innocent life forms on the earth? After all, it is only man that has raped and polluted the planet. It is only man that has killed for fun and for greed, placing a monetary value on the horns of animals or the fins of sharks. No, God didn't do this, this is on man himself, our greed and selfishness cost us and the animals we share our planet with the ultimate price.

Inside the briefing room Benjamin Young, as he now insisted he was to be called, was sat with Jonathan, Bruce and General Scott.

"Tell me it straight gentlemen," Benjamin said.

"Our atmosphere has now completely gone. There is no way back," Jonathan said.

"What happens next?"

"Soon we'll start to see the effects of solar radiation on the earth. The planet will start to be cooked and the solar winds will strip it bare. And that includes the oceans sir." Bruce answered.

"The earth will eventually resemble Mars sir." Jonathan added.

"And that's it, it ends here then. How long?" Benjamin asked.

"It's already begun. As for the oceans, days, weeks. We just don't know," Jonathan replied.

Benjamin sighed. "That'll be all."

Bruce and Jonathan stood and left the small situation room. Benjamin Young had one thing left he wanted to do before they were pulled, swept from the earth by the solar winds and scattered across the cosmos. He must confess to his wife. Tell her that it was his decision to push the Martialis project forward, and ultimately it was him that was responsible. If there was a God, he couldn't face him without first bearing his soul and asking for forgiveness from the one person from which it would count.

As a child, he had read in the Bible that the meek will inherit the earth. Is it feasible to think that we've being reading it wrong for all of these centuries? Could it be that as bacteria was the first living organism on earth that the expression, the meek will inherit the earth, refers to this first form of life? Jonathan had said that bacteria does exist in a vacuum, and on interplanetary bodies. Perhaps God has lost his patience with us and he's wiping the planet clean, like you would a computer hard drive. Perhaps God wants to start again? A fresh install. Mankind version 2.0.

It may also be, that there is no meaning of life, or God. And that our life has no more meaning than that of an amoeba.

Why should it be that mankind has a meaning of life and not the spider that hangs in the corner of a bedroom? Is it the arrogance of man that makes us believe that we are more important than any other living thing? Whatever the answers are, one thing now became clear to him. We are born, we live and we die, and we are not noticed or missed by the cosmos. We are in fact no more important than a single grain of sand on beach of trillions.

Epilogue
What's left behind

September 23rd, 2024. Mars Habitat. No time set

The Earth was now a lifeless rock. Mankind's cry of pain and anguish had gone unnoticed in the cosmos. Our screams unheard, like so many species before us, in the immensity of space.

After the death of the earth, mankind would live on with the twins born on Mars, to Mary and Joseph, September 23rd, 2023. Now a year old, they are called Adam and Eve.

Mankind's reign of planet Earth had come to its end. Long live mankind.

The End.

A thought from the author:

Imagine, if you will, that at some point in time you will be in the last hour of your life. And yet, you may not know that you are.